I0619877

CHAR   LIE

P
R
I
C
E

A   Novel by   Izaak David Diggs

© 2022 Izaak David Diggs
Released 13 August, 2022 (CFD)
ISBN 979-8-9864828-0-4
Cover design by Ike James

Forward

I have loved the *Dirty Harry* movies since I was a child. Some people see them as reactionary, embracing "right wing values and prejudices," that's not what I get from them. I always saw Harry Callahan as a loner, at odds with most people, seeing things others don't. In 2016 I was kicking around the idea of writing a "cop story." The original concept for *Charlie Price* was that he was a nephew of Harry Callahan or maybe even a secret son. Eventually I realized I was running towards a quagmire: *Dirty Harry* is a valuable franchise, they probably wouldn't want a lunatic like me mucking around in the canon, there would be all sorts of rules and potential lawsuits—
So Charlie Price became his own being, completely removed from the world of Harry Callahan.

At the time, I was working as a driver for a Major Car Rental Company. From late afternoon to after midnight I shuttled vehicles around the Portland, Oregon airport. When I was in disagreement with my boss, there were loads of spots to hide, secret areas beneath the parking garage. I'd find a spot to sit, pull out a tiny notebook I kept in my coat pocket, and work on this story. For a couple of weeks I had no idea how to start but one line got it rolling:
He was on the ground before the sound of the bullet left the air.
Five and a half years later, here we are.
I'm going to be honest, this story went in a number of directions: A billionaire benefactor of Charlie Price that was both benevolent and part of a vast conspiracy. A plot to blame an act of terrorism on area Muslims. A love interest for Charlie. None of these things felt right, honestly I have no idea how many times I

wrote out long bits only to discard them; the discards could be a book themselves...not a very good one, though.

Izaak
17 June, 2022

PART ONE: THE CHILDREN

The Children

He was on the ground before the sound of the bullet left the air. 9mm, somewhere off to the right---
The man rolled to the left, off the sidewalk and between parked cars. There was something sharp on the pavement--hopefully glass--that tore his pants and cut the skin on his leg.Wetness--blood; his favorite slacks were probably ruined. Knowing where the shot had come from the man withdrew his Ruger .357 and got into position. In five seconds he would be alive and the shooter would be dead. His index finger touched the side of the trigger---
It was just a boy, maybe eleven or twelve years old. Black. The gun in his hand jerked and there was another report. The shot was even further off than the first. It was probably the kid's first time with a gun; odds were that it would jam.
Odds, though, were not a guarantee.
There was a third shot but from a smaller gun, a .22 automatic, maybe a Beretta. A second boy was shooting at him. The two boys were laughing and shouting curse words at the man with the torn pants.
"I'm a cop! Put those guns down!"
The words burst from him automatically; even as he was yelling at them the cop understood that the words would have no value to the children: They probably knew that he was a cop and they weren't going to put their guns down. A fourth shot, this one from the 9mm. The cop reholstered his sidearm; it went against every instinct but shooting the children was unthinkable. The problem was when *other* cops showed up: They would not run the risk of restraint and there would be two dead kids, Black ones. Riots would follow and more people would be hurt and killed.

That was unacceptable to the cop with the torn pants: He needed to neutralize the kids without lethal force.

Did they have extra clips? Unknown.

Would they know how to load extra clips? Also unknown. Kids picked up things from TV and movies; that could include loading guns.

The man's palm hovered over the gun holster; it felt wrong to leave his hand empty. He worked on distracting his own anxiety with the details of the situation. No one was going to call the cops in that neighborhood but a patrol car was due. It'd roll right past where the man was bleeding into his favorite pants. He knew the officer on patrol: Young. Eager to see some action. Possibly racist. The man knew how the encounter would play out, that it would get ugly fast. The kids would have to be lured away before the patrol car rolled past.

There was a vacant apartment complex a block to the east--

It would get the boys out of sight of the patrol car...

It would also be a good place for an ambush.

Locals: Seeing a cop running in alone, looking to get revenge for all the bad things the police had done to them over the years.

Locals: Ones who knew how to shoot and reload guns.

It was a risk the cop would have to take.

Another shot from the .22, it came close enough that the man could see where the slug pocked the earth.

"Save your bullets! Save your bullets!" The older boy yelled at the smaller one.

It was a smart call; it also lowered the odds of the child seeing the end of the day.

The cop ran a serpentine pattern down the street close to the parked cars; the kids were terrible shots but even terrible shots get lucky. He could feel the blood on his leg growing tacky---when had his last tetanus shot been? Probably when he was in the Army. The ruined neighborhood could have been anywhere in the world. A battered Corolla pushed him years back; that type of car was all over the other place, the last city he had heard gunshots out in the open.

"Don't shoot them, I think it's just kids."

Yes, he had said that—then. *Then* was forcing its way in, relegating *now* to a corner. The yelling of the children brought him back as the man jogged into an abandoned apartment complex.

Are you sure you are back? Are you really sure?

Yes, he knew the complex, it had burned the same month he had made Inspector: A tweaker had fallen asleep with a cigarette; nothing had been left of her but some charred meat. The apartments had been a total loss. Most of the windows were broken out and the doors kicked in. In the present, The cop drew his Ruger and appraised every shadow and corner. There was a calmness with the gun in his hand, a comfort brought on by the weight of the revolver. *Low2Dipz Ryder* had been sprayed poorly in blue paint on a cinderblock wall and some brown birds were pecking in a pool of sunshine---what were they eating? Locals *had* to have heard the shots; all it would take would be one busy body with a cell phone calling an uncle or an older sister or a cousin; an armed crew would roll up and things would get ugly fast---

Finches, the birds were probably finches. Finches or sparrows.

The man didn't want to involve anyone else but understood he needed another brain and pair of eyes. The smells of burnt wood and urine had a familiarity that made him swoon. Burnt wood, urine, armed children---memories attempting to take over his senses.

Now was in the corner, about to slip out the door.

Don't shoot them, I think it's just kids.

He went from having the Ruger in his hand to an M4; he went from being alone to having two shadows.

"I don't give a fuck, they can kill you same as an adult can here," one of his guards said that, spit the words out as if they tasted bad.

Wandering through ruins---had it gotten hotter? Had the smells changed?

Children laughing and yelling. The words were in English; he was back in the present.

"This is no time to lose your shit," the cop muttered to himself. Why was he thinking of the past? It had been years...

Was he in a strong enough mental state to deal with the kids? What if he just ran off? Would the kids give up on the game or would they wait until patrol came by and take pot shots at the prowler? Unknown.

A call to prayer somewhere off to his left; his shadow was getting anxious but he wouldn't let it happen again---

Again? How could there have been a before?

This was no time for memories to take over; the man focused on the present, on keeping the two boys stalking him alive. A plan was taking shape in his mind: He reached in his coat, withdrew his phone with his left hand, and dialed a number. The voice on the other end brought him a comfort that he understood was potentially both complicated and dangerous.

"Charlie---what's up?"

Mendez knew he hated phones and only used them when he had to. It was before his shift so she probably understood that his call wasn't work related---not really, not officially, at least. Charlie explained the situation and what he needed in twenty-three words. She responded with two words: Ten minutes.

The kids had followed Charlie in and were hunting him. Their laughter was a reminder that they were just children messing around---
Children with guns playing games they didn't understand the consequences of.

Don't shoot them, I think it's just kids.

At that time, in another country, he had understood that his shadow would ignore that request: Charlie was his responsibility; a man with good intentions who was naive about being out in the field, his shadow had said as much over drinks; drowning sorrows that had learned how to swim.

Don't shoot them, I think it's just kids.

But his shadow wouldn't listen; the past had already been made, a monster stepping from behind walls or through doors to taunt him.

The weapon in Charlie's hand was a Ruger .357 again; the cop forced himself to reholster it. Maybe he could save the children that day but what about in the coming weeks and months? Too many kids---in bad neighborhoods and good ones---were left to figure out stuff on their own. All Charlie had was that day and on that day he was determined to keep them alive. A radio was playing old R & B nearby. At the end of the third song Charlie circled back to the entrance of the complex. He was purposefully clumsy, making noise to keep the boys aware of his location.
Had that last song been the Spinners or the Temptations?
Lilacs were growing wild in some spilled dirt. There had been flowers in the past as well: Not Lilacs, Price saw opium poppies in his memories but that wasn't right. One moment they were yellow flowers and the next blue. His shadow was making a bitter taste face as he aimed.

In the present, Charlie rolled the fabric of his pants between his left thumb and index finger; a wool blend, not the material of fatigues---

What had that been? Some sort of cotton-poly blend? He would have to look it up when he got home.

I am in America. I am a cop. I am not going back there.

But the beast had come around a corner, smiling and nodding. He liked to think he was strong but it was stronger, stronger than every man in the world who tried to lie to himself.

Fuck that. Focus on the feel of the wool, that is real. Focus---focus or they die.

The cop had to remind them of his presence, he had to keep the boys in the game or they might leave the building. If they left the building with guns they could die. The cop would put himself in the same corridor as the children. He would jump out and wave just long enough to pump fresh blood into the game but not long enough to spill his own blood on the weed gagged cement. It was a risk that he had to take.

The vest was exactly where he had told Mendez to leave it. Charlie thought of the last time he had seen her and wondered if he had done the right thing. The man in the bulletproof vest pulled out his phone and called the same number he had called thirteen minutes earlier.

"I'm at the entrance. They're maybe two hundred meters away."

"Meters?" She sounded confused, maybe not awake.

"Sorry, *yards*," he clarified. "I hear them, they're off to my left." It was a bad idea but it was the only one he had and time was running out. Even in the space of fifteen minutes the cop could see patterns in the boys' behavior, the way they hunted him through the complex. They were scared, especially the smaller one, but determined to shoot the White Cop. Maybe it was to impress older kids.

No "maybe," that was definitely it.

Charlie stepped into a breezeway and saw them; the guns looked absurd in their small hands.

"Hey!" He yelled.

The smaller one dropped his gun and looked terrified. The older one looked over at Charlie and the cop saw something he didn't like. The eyes: He had seen those eyes too many times in his life. The cop understood the brain behind those eyes and any optimism he had faded. The older boy fired a shot and then a second. Charlie moved with each one, willing himself not to dive to safety. The smaller boy cowered like a dog that had been beaten repeatedly. The set of his mouth and the twist of his face revealed that he was seconds away from tears.

"Pick up your gun, shoot the motherfucker!" The older child yelled.

And then he aimed again and Charlie understood the next shot would probably be true---

And then Mendez was there grabbing the arm that ended at the gun. The shot went wild and masked the snapping sound but not the shriek that followed it. Charlie rushed in and kicked the .22 away from the smaller boy; the tears had arrived and the child had wet his pants. The older boy was cradling his arm and shrieking.

"He twisted when I grabbed his arm," Mendez apologized. "I think it's broken."

She looked ashamed and angry; maybe she was angry at Charlie for calling her and putting her in the position where she had to break childrens' arms. Charlie looked down at the 9mm---where had the kid gotten it?

And then the child was not whimpering and cradling his arm, the child was still and silent in a spreading pool of blood. The Beast was at Charlie's side, chuckling and showing him photographs of the past, a past he had allowed to happen.

The cop focused on the way Mendez's hair framed her face and the smell of the smaller boy's urine to return to the present. One of the brown birds had alighted on a window. It was definitely a sparrow. Price pulled his mobile out of his coat to call the incident in. The words were there, he could see them, it was up to his mouth to shape them and let them out. Three words: The code and the address. How could three words be a mountain?

"Want me to call it in?" Mendez had been watching him.

"I got it," he said softly.

The phone call was just the first obstacle. A few minutes after the call ended cops would show up and look him in the face and there would be conversations and people probing him for clues and replies. Charlie held his phone out with his eyes closed, somethings never got easier.

Aftermath

The older boy with the broken arm was named Charlie Russell.
His name is Charlie Russell, he's only eleven years old.
An indignant woman had yelled that at the cops when they
loaded the boy into the ambulance. They didn't see two children
alive because of a cop's restraint, they just saw one of their kids
who had his arm broken by the police. Things were still ugly and
probably would be for some time. Often sometimes means
forever.

Charlie Russell---the cop turned the name over in his mind as he
walked home. A uniform offered him a ride but the confines of a
car was the last thing he needed. The Beast was on his heels, a
ghost with body odor and insistent words; pushing photographs
in Charlie's face that the cop endeavored to ignore. The sounds of
heavy machinery in the distance; the big new project down by the
river that had been going on for a couple of years. The town had
been quiet for decades until people had realized there was money
to be made: Land was bought up. Houses were torn down.
Promises of a bright future passed through Arizona White smiles.

It was a nine block walk from the abandoned complex to his
house. The streets were quiet aside from the homeless people
going through bins. A couple of them were talking and laughing,
the voices were in street English then Pashto.
*I am losing my shit---is it the stress of what just happened? I haven't
thought about Afghanistan in ten years at least.*
Once home, the cop changed his pants. There was a hole but
maybe it could be mended. He fretted over children with guns;
they were all over the world, moving down dirt streets and

smoothly paved boulevards. Unable to find peace, he cued "As" by Stevie Wonder on his stereo and sat on the arm of his couch with his eyes closed.

Peace was a gift that would be reclaimed...eventually: Charlie knew there would be trouble for his actions. Anxiety built as he changed his pants. He knew that he had done the right thing but very few of his co-workers would see it that way, maybe none. His belt was starting to peel apart, it always seemed to happen to his belts---
It had to be the stress of subduing the armed children that was bringing back the past; intellectually, Charlie understood that he had experienced trauma and it would keep coming back all his life. The children being gunned down in Afghanistan wasn't what troubled him, though, it was part of his memory, the determination not to let children be killed *again*.
Again? That had been his first tour as a soldier, there was no *before*---
There is. That's the problem, I remember what I was thinking and feeling twenty years ago and I had been determined not to let children die again but...
What was the before? What was his memory blocking?

A text from the Captain came in as Charlie buckled his belt. The tone of the message was friendly, breezy even, but urgent: Please come within the hour. A crow called from nearby and the cop went to the window to try and find it. The bird was on the wires over the sidewalk. Charlie wanted to spend all day like that: In the calm of his own yard. Watching birds. Maybe playing piano. He could take his phone to the back porch and smash it with a hammer---

Then the message---and, in turn, the outside world---wouldn't exist.

If only it were that easy.

The bird turned its head and seemed to be looking right at him.

Charlie grabbed his keys and walked out the door.

The boys had been squeezing triggers, the boys had *been* triggers. Charlie sat in the driver's seat of his car and fell into the cracks in the dashboard. There was no mystery as to why the past had been intruding after a few years of peace; the past is something that never dies, only sleeps.

I can't let it happen again. Again. *That wasn't the first time...why do I feel that?*

The cop pulled himself out of the cracks and cranked the starter. The car shuddered as the engine roared to life. He ran his hand over the vinyl shift knob and then forced himself back into the moment.

The administrative section of the station had never felt right to him, it felt more like an insurance office than a police station: Shades of beige. Cubicle walls. The smell of burnt popcorn in the break room. Charlie was aware of people looking at him and whispering as he walked between the cubicles—he worked on forcing himself to believe it was just his imagination. There were too many corridors with T-intersections and he got lost. A Major in khakis nearly ran into him. "Brueller" was what her name tag said---

She knows that we were up north. This is where the court martial begins.

And then she was a heavy set woman in a beige pantsuit. Price turned around and walked back the way he had come.

The Captain had Charlie wait in his reception area long enough to endure three soft rock classics coming over the speakers. Sitting there, the cop became preoccupied with the dark stained door as he prepared himself for the conversation. He made a game of remembering the names of the bands; only the second one stumped him. As the third song ended a Lieutenant with a ruler straight part in his brown hair walked out; the face was familiar but the name eluded him.

"You can go in, Inspector," he smiled a grim smile at Price.

The name of the Lieutenant had an "r" on the end--Barker? Marver?

He had forgotten to look up the material their uniforms had been made of.

Walking in the office Charlie was overwhelmed by the smell of Axe body spray. The Captain's morning routine: A workout and shower before work, Axe playing a starring role in the shower. His superior was sitting behind his desk with a friendly smile that was clearly a mask. A soft looking Asian woman from HR sat in a chair facing the door. Her bare legs looked mottled: Psoriasis? A birth defect? Her blouse was ill fitting, all straining buttons and stiff fabric. She probably didn't know how to shop for clothes, maybe she rushed through picking out clothes because the crowds in shops made her anxious. That possibility made her likable.

"Price, what's the good word?"

The Captain's voice was big and shiny, a voice for selling products. Charlie had no idea what the product was, he just wanted to get through with it and deal with whatever punishment he faced.

"This is Yon from HR," Captain added. "She's just sitting in on our conversation."

15

The Asian woman nodded politely but looked bored or maybe half awake.

Was it psoriasis or was it eczema? What was the difference between the two?

The Captain stopped smiling and looked sad, another mask. This one fit better; for all Price knew it was his real face.

"So, Inspector Price, we need to have a career conversation."

A meaningful pause. His boss was trying to meet Price's eyes and Charlie knew that he was supposed to meet the gaze but his instincts kept turning his head to the side. After a few seconds the Captain gave up and continued speaking.

"You really let the team down this morning and I just wanted to see where your head's at. I am working to understand what I can do with this coaching opportunity you've given me."

Price shifted in his seat. Why was he there? What was the point of his being there? The Captain had already made his mind up and had probably already emailed his opinions to Internal Affairs. Charlie struggled to keep a scowl from forming on his face but in the end the battle was lost.

"I was trying to keep two children from getting killed," he said, clenching to keep from letting his anger out his mouth.

The Captain opened a drawer in his desk and looked in it for a couple of seconds. What was in that drawer? Why had he chosen that moment to look in it?

It was the sort of thing that could drive Price mad if he let it. His boss was trying to look thoughtful but he could sense anger crackling at the edges; an enemy at the gates testing reinforced steel and locks.

"I get that," his superior said. "But we have the means to neutralize people without killing them. Bean Bag guns," the Captain smiled and winked at Yon. "Bean Bag guns are *awesome*."

The words were there but so was a disgust Price's voice wouldn't bother concealing. He gave himself a few seconds to distract his contempt with the memory of the crow on the wire.

"That's Malston's patrol; we know he's trigger happy, especially when it comes to Blacks, and he might not have waited for a non lethal solution to the situation."

The Captain looked thoughtful and nodded. Part of him clearly wanted to stand up and yell, Charlie imagined the yelling man inside the captain as a shadow on the wall that demanded to take form. There were rumors around the precinct that the Captain had been verbally abusive in the past and had consequently been forced to attend anger management courses. Yelled profanities and threats would have been preferable to Charlie.

"I believe I understand your reasons and I know your heart was in the right place," the boss said. "Nevertheless, you made a bad decision. Those kids had guns and you allowed them to continue firing which jeopardized public safety."

Charlie thought of the neighborhood---*his* neighborhood---and how there were always drug deals and violence but a call to 911 got the caller nothing but a wait that could be hours. The conversation was pointless and he was itching for it to be over. There was a small coffee stain near one of the legs of the desk. It was an odd place to spill coffee: If a cup had been knocked over the overhang of the desk should have taken the liquid further out. Maybe the spill was from when the desk had been in another location.

Why are you focusing on such trivial things? Hold it together, your job is at stake.

"Captain, I would like to think both of us live in the real world," Charlie said carefully. "We both know there would be riots if those kids had been shot---"

His boss held his hands up and allowed his smile to fade.

"Price, *enough*. You let the team down and you put a colleague, a *pregnant* colleague, in harm's way. How can you justify that?"
Charlie was looking over at a picture of the Captain with the Mayor. It looked like it had been taken at a picnic. Big smiles, the Captain awkwardly putting a hand on the Mayor's shoulder. And then, like a double exposure, the vision of Charlie Russell and the younger boy and what kids that small looked like after they'd been shot up.
And then: Two different brown boys, one resting a hand on a piece of wood carved and painted to look like an AK-47.
The cop knew not to share that with his boss or HR; they would use the memory against him.
"Dawn Mendez was following the orders of a ranking officer, Captain; I hope you'll take that into consideration."
His boss looked over at Yon and they exchanged a look Charlie couldn't interpret.
"Don't worry about your partner, Price," The Captain said.
"Worry about yourself and your future here. We're placing you on administrative leave until we reach a resolution."
"Do you need my service weapon and badge?"
The anger was no longer there; the Captain seemed genuinely at peace.
"Yes. Sorry, boss."
Charlie pulled the 9mm he carried out and placed it on the desk.
That was no big deal; he only carried it because he was required to. Laying his badge next to the gun was the troubling part; *that* had meaning to him. Yon pulled her phone out of her coat pocket and took pictures of the two items. The Captain smiled and nodded at her. The smile left his face before he turned back to Charlie.
"I hate doing this but you've painted me in a corner," he said regretfully.

Price looked down at the coffee stain and tried to ignore how the two other people in the room were staring at him. When would he be let go? When would all the meaningless words and the staring end?

"Am I dismissed?" He asked.

"Sure." The Captain said softly.

Administrative Leave

Administrative leave was a netherworld, it could be days or it could be months. Price knew he had done the right thing but that knowledge did nothing for his frustration. Why couldn't people in authority see that his actions were the right ones? How had they risen through the ranks if they couldn't see something so obvious? Dawn could handle herself; he wouldn't have called her if she couldn't. The problem was that the Captain couldn't imagine those boys dead, he hadn't seen the things Charlie had and was lucky for it. Passing a cubicle, a photo of a smiling child in a corridor---

Then: Both black boys dead in different corridors of the abandoned complex. The smaller one with a large hole in his torso and blood and gore fanned out behind where he fell. The other one missing most of his head. Dawn, fearing for Charlie's safety, had called for backup and the children had been gunned down. That alternate reality was what the Captain couldn't see and Charlie couldn't stop seeing. The cop jammed a thumbnail into his index finger until the pain brought *now* back into focus.

A couple of the patrol cops were standing around a lifted Dodge truck parked next to Price's old Mercedes. They were talking loudly and laughing about something. A crow cawed from nearby, Charlie stopped to study it for a moment.

"Hey, Price!"

One of the cops had stepped in the way of Charlie's path to the driver's door. He was smiling but it was toothy and edged, the smile of a predator. Were his teeth that straight naturally or he had spent a lot of time in orthodontist chairs as a child?

"You get fired, bro?" The patrol cop asked.

The beat cop was a head taller than Price and built up, probably from obsessive workouts and supplements that may or may not have been legal. Price shook his head.

"That was some crazy ass shit, bro." The cop smiled. "Using a pregnant woman for a shield."

So *that* was what they thought; what they thought didn't matter but the lack of a precise narrative bothered Charlie. He didn't want to go through the trouble of making words for them but hoped it would be the simplest way out of the situation.

"Gotta go, guys," he said.

The big cop was still blocking Price's path to the driver's side door, no longer smiling.

"This ain't the army, bro." He said.

Charlie assessed the situation: Kicking the other cop somewhere painful would definitely get him fired---fired and possibly beat down. Did he care? Did he *really*? Or, was this an opportunity to escape being a cop presenting itself?

"Yo, watch out, bro," the other cop smirked. "He may be a little dude but he probably knows all sorts of crazy army killer shit."

The one blocking Charlie's path pretended to be scared and stepped out of the way.

"You get on home in your antique car, Price," he said, looking over at his buddy with a smirk.

Charlie could have squeezed around him and gotten in his car but something had been triggered. Bullies, he remembered them making his life a hell as a kid but he wasn't a child anymore. Charlie was watching the cop's fingers, imagining just grabbing one and twisting until it snapped: The feel of rough warm skin. The hand pulling back an instant too late. The finger resisting the movement then giving abruptly. Watching the face change from smugness to surprise and pain and then fury---

And then it would begin.

The two men faced each other and the parking lot became silent, even the crow was quiet.

"Come on, Price; we're going to be late," a voice behind him said. A slight man with a large mustache had appeared at the passenger side of the car.

Charlie recognized him but couldn't place him---

Leaving? The bully would win as he had probably won more times than he had deserved. The man standing on the other side of the car was watching him, sending something his way---

"Charlie, don't go there," the man with the mustache said.

Who was he? Neither of the other cops seemed to acknowledge the presence of the man with the mustache. *He's a friend*---that's all Charlie knew, that and his instincts were telling him to listen to the man standing across the Mercedes. Price squeezed past the cop and opened the driver side door. Leaning across the car, Charlie opened the passenger door and smelled lilacs. The two uniforms were looking in the car and chuckling like dogs that only know how to growl. Bullies, they probably made thoughtless jokes and smacked the vulnerable around back in school; Charlie Price in another life---

"Just drive, Price," his passenger said firmly.

The man in the other seat sounded tired or maybe bored. Price pulled out of the lot and headed in the general direction of his house.

"What were you going to do, Charlie? I saw your face; it wasn't a good face."

His passenger's mustache fascinated him; it looked like a prop from a Western or gay porn.

"Where are we going?" The words came easy, without a war. There was something about his passenger that always him feel calm.

"I'd say a drink but since you're sober now I'll settle for five minutes in your car," the passenger said. "You can drop me back at the station when we're done."

"Okay---"

Gilbert Franks. Why do I get the feeling we're related, like he's a cousin or something?

It made no sense, but the feeling was strong. Charlie was curious why Franks had chosen that moment to appear. The other man looked down at his pants, smoothed them with his hands, and then looked at the driver.

"Those boys reminded you of what happened in the War, didn't they?"

Dead boys---*something happened, I failed but I cannot see it. Those boys died in that apartment complex but my mind is blocking the truth.*

"Yeah, ones their age. Afghani. The soldiers I was with acted impulsively."

Gilbert seemed to be looking at the cracks in the dash.

"We're spoiled by our cars, aren't we?"

Franks said that softly before looking over at Price and continuing.

"You shouldn't have called Mendez, that was a mistake."

Charlie grabbed the steering wheel and squeezed it to release the pressure in his head.

"Charlie," Gilbert said softly. "I know you did what you did to save those boys and who knows how many people who would have died in the riots that would have followed; it was right but it was also wrong."

Forms were going up in a vacant lot they were passing---what was going to be built there? It was probably judged for mixed-use judging by the buildings on the block.

"I'm thinking of getting out of this," Price said. "Why do this job if you can't do it the way it should be done?"

A block passed. The silence in the car grew heavier but not uncomfortable.

"So, what has all your work to become an Inspector been for?" Gilbert asked. "You've dealt with this sort of situation before, why is it getting to you now?"

A light ahead turned yellow, the brakes squeaked a little when applied.

"I don't know," Price said. "For some reason I was having really weird feelings...like those kids being killed in Afghanistan wasn't the first time, like I had been over there before which doesn't make any sense."

Franks said nothing in return, his expression was neutral.

"And when I was in the Captain's office I was noticing *everything* including a coffee stain on the rug I hadn't picked up on before."

The light turned green, Price drove on slowly.

"If I am having a breakdown or something...maybe I'm not cut out for this job anymore.

Charlie had been making a series of right turns and now they were back at the precinct; he pulled up to the curb.

"It's going to be okay," Franks smiled at him with a hand on the door handle. "Maybe you just needed some time off."

"I could really use some advice about this," Price said.

Did that sound harsh? His tone of voice had been harder than he had intended. The man with the mustache didn't appear offended or any other emotion for that matter.

"We're gonna get through this," Gilbert smiled under his mustache.

He climbed out and leaned against the door to give Charlie one last piece of advice.

"Use this suspension to your advantage."

What Military Uniforms Are Made Out Of

Fifty percent cotton and fifty percent nylon.

The Abandon Car and the Spinet

The trip from the police station to his house took eleven minutes in light traffic. Price had made it in nine when running late for work but when it was rush hour it could take---
What was before?
And what was his relationship with Gilbert Franks? He recognized the face, knew they were close, maybe blood relatives---
The boys with the guns, it was fucking with his head, no elegant way to put it—there had been a desperation to save them because he hadn't saved the ones before. The world felt different, his anxiety did that.
But I saved them...I'm pretty sure.

There was a new stripped car on Price's street. No plates, no wheels, the VIN numbers had probably been scraped. Behind the car was a pile of bursting garbage bags and broken furniture. More than once he had rented a pickup to clear the road of trash. His enthusiasm for the project, always slight, had diminished but his determination was still strong; it was a grim determination but it had a steady pulse. Pulling in the drive the cop had it down to a science exactly where to stop so he could open the gate; line the side mirror lined with where the edge of the sidewalk met what had been a lawn. His eyes moved down the street to the stripped car.
Then: The feeling of a rifle in his hands. The smell of garbage burning, dark skinned men with beards...
Now: No, there was no metal in his hands, he was home, whatever that meant.

Price drove the Mercedes to the end of the drive and closed the gate. The front windows were always shuttered; neighborhood kids knew where "The Cop" lived and had broken a window shortly after he had moved in. It was the worst part of town and Price couldn't imagine living anywhere else, a war zone. The gunshots he heard every night were comforting in ways he couldn't explain or even understand himself.

The battered spinet in the living room had been dumped two streets over. Local kids had laughed when he pushed it home. Unlocking the front door he thought of that day, their mocking faces. How many of them would die because of a bullet? *Then, now*, it was both places. He thought of their faces still or in one last mask of agony, their bodies riddled. The smell of gunpowder and blood in the air---
Price walked to the piano, sat down, and played until the sound of the notes had smoothed his anxiety. The piano tuner had refused to come over until Charlie promised him a "police escort." He was in his sixties with hair slicked back with grease. The tuner had smelled of Old Spice covering up dirty clothes.

The spinet was one of the few pieces in the house: A simple table with two chairs. A bookcase overflowing with books. A dresser. A mattress in one of the bedrooms on pallets taken from the back of a grocery store. A few of Celeste's framed pictures on a wall. That was enough. Charlie went to one of the pictures and looked at it closely: Afghani children, smiling shyly. Looking at the picture reminded him of the kids his minders had shot---
And *before*, whatever that meant.

Memories of a Jail

A memory: Hands smacking his shoulders through his shirt as then pushing him into the concrete wall of his cell; the violence of the prisoner's situation becoming real. The energy was all sparks and jagged pieces, anger and a physical manifestation of that anger turned on another human being. The prisoner understood that he was powerless and in a deeper trouble than he had been in a long time.

"Did you hear me, son?" A loud male voice, slight twang. The smell of chewing tobacco and cheap aftershave.

Yes, he heard the man, but the words weren't there to respond---the words were locked away somewhere. Nodding his head hadn't satisfied the guard, the man with the gun expected words.

"Yes..." The prisoner said.

Another hard shove, his head bounced off the cinderblocks---how had his skull not fractured?

"Yes, *what*?" The guard roared.

One word, three small letters---was it so much to ask? It was clear his life depended on it. The guard was reaching for his zipper; who knew what that meant. No, the prisoner understood exactly what it meant, the zipper had come down before.

"Yes, sir," he said.

The guard was still staring at him, still touching the front of his pants.

"I hear you have some fancy lawyer coming here," he chewed on the words casually. "Let me tell you, your fancy lawyer can't do shit. This is Texas. We don't stand around when people break our laws. Hear?"

Everything was locked up. The words had gone even deeper; why couldn't he depend on them? The guard was close enough that the prisoner could nearly taste his smells: Skoal. Dial soap. Some garish cologne, probably an Old Spice knock off. The hot dogs he had for lunch. Something big was pushing against the zipper, something growing. The guard had shaken his heavy penis through the bars the day before. It had been a threat then, maybe it was about to become more than a threat—what would that do to his insides? The guard would probably be rough.

No, he *definitely* would be rough.

"Yes, sir," the prisoner said.

Nothing about the guard changed. Wasn't the second word what he wanted? It was probably just a game, letting the prisoner see the exit then shoving him out of view of it. His penis looked smaller, though, that was a good thing, and he was backing out of the cell.

"How did a pussy like you ever drive a truck?" The guard shook his head. "Thought that was a man's job."

Was he expecting an answer? No, he was locking the door and walking away.

The Fat Chance

The mostly plain walls of the cop's house were a problem; they gave the memories something to ricochet off. They were ricocheting and striking him over and over with greater velocity, going from bad places to even worse places. How long had he been pacing? Going to the laptop he saw that three songs had played. It was time to get out; the memories couldn't ricochet so easily outside, there was more of a chance of them shooting out into the atmosphere and disappearing.
No, the memories have only begun to fuck with me.

It was eleven in the morning but Price wore the Ruger out of habit. He had tried walking around unarmed one time but it had been very uncomfortable. The cop stopped under a spreading tree to listen to birds arguing. Where was he going? He stood in a ring of birdshit thinking about the big cop and the little boys and for some reason it led him back to Celeste.
The tavern, that was where he was walking to.

A Mexican teenager was messing around under the hood of a battered Toyota. There was the sound of a wrench hitting metal--- it reminded Price of the sound of the guard hitting his club against the bars to get his attention. In his memory, Charlie went back to his cell but...it had changed. Instead of cement the walls were rough stones and the floor was earth with hay tossed on it.
The only time I was in jail was in Texas, this memory...is illogical.
No, it was a valid memory, a real one that he had only just recalled, had been sunk in a deep body of water but for some reason had broken the surface. A crow called from nearby, scolding other birds or maybe Price himself.

"At least it's a beautiful day to lose my mind," he sighed.

The Fat Chance was a shabby bar in a shabby neighborhood. Every time the owner tried to spruce it up the regulars complained so he gave up, leaving the toilets in a state of nastiness and the naughyde in the booths torn with dirty stuffing too weary to burst out. Price habitually checked out the entire bar in the moments it took to close the door behind him. The owner, also out of habit, had looked up from getting a can of Rainer to see who had let a few seconds of sunshine in.

"How about that fucking beer, Chrissy?"

The voice belonged to one of the barflies and the words were more croaked than spoken. He was somewhere between thirty and a hundred with a permanent sunburn. The other regulars laughed. A couple of nervous hipsters at a side table looked even more nervous. Another regular, one with a black eye, turned on his stool to see who had come in.

"Watch out, Joey, it's Chris's cop friend!"

More laughter. The hipsters were looking at each other and clearly debating whether or not to flee. Price took a stool and Chris walked over to him.

"Drinking at eleven in the morning, Inspector?" He asked.

"I'm not an Inspector."

Chris walked over to the portion of the shelf where the whiskeys were kept and looked over at his friend expectantly.

"Glenlivit," Charlie said quietly.

"Funny, I was going to guess Johnny Walker Black."

He poured two fingers and handed it across the bar. There was a paperback with a blue cover on the shelf; Price motioned towards it.

"What are you reading?"

"It's a strange book, strange but interesting: Four people driving across a desert but it's really hot, 130 degrees."

He looked thoughtful, pulled a rag out and started wiping the counter.

"It's getting hotter all over the world, even here we'll have more and more days over a hundred degrees."

The bartender returned to the present and focused on his friend.

"Back to the present: Why are you not an Inspector?"

Charlie told the briefest version of the story as possible, leaving out all the memories that had been coming back and the appearance of Gilbert Franks.

"I heard about that, kid had his arm snapped." One of the Black barflies, his voice was irritated but his face appeared resigned.

"The other cop didn't know her own strength," Price explained.

"Mendez?" Chris was pouring well tequila into a glass. "Your new partner?"

"Yes and don't jinx her like that."

Price took a sip from his drink and understood that the whiskey was a mistake; alcohol would only complicate the anxiety and irritation he felt. Chris had been watching his face and set a glass of water next to the tumbler.

"Is this one of the days you consider quitting the force?" The bartender asked.

Charlie picked up the glass and savored the smell of the whiskey and the way it captured the overhead light. He set it down.

"What else would I do?" That question more posed to himself than his friend.

Chris walked into the kitchen and returned with a plateful of tots. He took them over to the hipsters who had been reaching for their coats.

"Don't be scared kids, we're all nice here," he forced a smile. The bartender didn't smile out of habit but forced himself on occasion.

"Nice and drunk," Joey sighed. The other regulars laughed. Charlie winced. Three words, thoughtlessly thrown out, worthless yet weighted. He knew that if he looked over he would see his own head on the barfly's body.

"Maybe you could be a teacher," Chris said thoughtfully once back behind the bar. "Didn't you consider being a high school teacher back in the day?"

Price had, until he found out the job was nearly as political as being a cop; the idea of passing students so they could stay on a sports team was unthinkable.

"I know I made the right decision," Charlie said softly.

Chris took a bottle of catsup over to the hipsters.

"Obviously your captain didn't think so," he said

Price picked up the whiskey glass, he wanted a sip badly.

No, the idea of drinking it was disgusting and the implications of drinking it made him anxious.

"You live around here, you know what would have happened if those kids got killed," Charlie said.

The Black barfly looked over at Price. When their eyes met the barfly nodded. There was something about the regular, maybe he had been in one of the Gulf Wars.

"We both know it was right, Charlie," Chris said. "But you didn't make a *career decision*."

Something he already knew. Why had he come to the bar? He should have known Chris would give him a lecture.

"This isn't my career, this is my job," Price said.

The bartender laughed. One of the regulars raised his hand and Chris grabbed the well whiskey and poured three fingers.

"Could I get an ice cube, too?" The regular asked.

"I'll slip one in, don't let Price see, though; he's a snob."

"Fuck him, unless he's paying for my drink---" the regular growled.

"Then you'll fuck him?" Joey again.

The barflies laughed. The hipsters were too busy eating to be worried. The bartender walked back down to Charlie's stool and leaned across the bar.

"Face it, this is what you do. What are the options? Driving a truck again? Going back into the Army?"

Price just raised an eyebrow. Chris looked around the bar, six customers, about the most he ever had in the place.

"As your friend I am telling you to either play ball or find another gig or sell your house and wander the earth."

Charlie picked up the tumbler and swished the whiskey around the glass.

"Wander the earth, not a bad idea."

"You ever consider being a bodyguard?" Chris said. "Deal with just one asshole and get paid well?"

"Nah, this is what I'm supposed to do, I just have to work this out."

Was it really? Or were they just empty words tossed out like balloons to keep the conversation from getting too weighted? The Black vet had raised his hand to get the bartender's attention. Charlie pulled a five from his wallet and left it on the bar.

One Day Soon You'll Have to Choose

Charlie knew all the cars on his street that belonged to his neighbors and the Oldsmobile wasn't one of them: Early nineties Delta 88. Worn paint. Cluttered interior. The cop paused on his stoop with keys in hand to study the car. The wheels looked stock so it probably wasn't a gangsta or a wanna be, no bass signature from over-amped hip hop. It was creeping, though, like the driver had a mission on Price's street. The car pulled to the curb. Charlie put his keys back in his pocket as the driver climbed from behind his seat: Heavy. Between six-one and six-three. White. Somewhere in his fifties. Droopy mustache that was more salt than pepper. Mustache Man walked to his trunk, opened it, and pulled out a bag of trash. He added it to the pile next to the stripped car without bothering to look around. Charlie walked out and closed the distance between them. There was no hesitation; he felt that the words were close and wouldn't fail him, something had forced his discomfort away. Probably disgust or irritation. Did he identify himself as a cop? No, best confront the man as a property owner defending his neighborhood. Mustache Man didn't bolt when he saw Price coming, he stared back and closed his trunk hard.

"I know what you're thinkin'," the man with the Olds said.

"Listen...I'm a vet: I can't afford trash service, boss."

Price said nothing and continued walking until he was a few feet from the Oldsmobile.

"You ain't gonna start somethin', are ya?" Mustache Man sighed. He had pulled a pack of cigarettes out and lit one. Parliaments. Mr. Mustache didn't seem nervous or shameful or anything but hungry for that cigarette; maybe it was because he had a few inches and fifty pounds on Charlie or maybe he had a piece tucked in his back waistband. No, Price had watched him walk from the driver's seat to the trunk when he bent down to get the trash---there was no gun in his waistband. If he had an ankle holster it would probably be a struggle for him to grab it giving the cop time and consequently options.

"It's just trash," the big man said. "Niggers are used to living with the stuff."

Price just stared at him. His jacket was open, if Mustache Man was paying attention he'd see the gun.

"Open your trunk," the cop said quietly but firmly.

Mustache Man tilted his head like a dog hearing an unfamiliar sound.

"Whatcha gonna do if I don't? I see the antique under your jacket---you gonna shoot me?"

Another long drag, there was curiosity in his eyes now. Charlie weighed his options but didn't break his gaze.

"You see that house down there?" The cop pointed to a pale blue house, one of the few well kept places on the street.

Mustache Man looked from Price to the house and back to Price. "What about it?" He asked warily.

Charlie pulled out his phone and took a shot of the Oldsmobile's backplate.

"Hey!" The outsider half yelled, half whined.

There wasn't the usual struggle and calculation; the words were coming easy to Price and it felt good.

"Yolanda Jimenez lives in that house," the cop explained. "Nice woman, works at the DMV. Her younger brother Miguel is not so nice; he especially hates old white racists."

It took a few seconds for Mustache Man to figure out what Price was saying. The curiosity in his eyes was replaced by contempt.

"One day soon you'll have to choose, son," he said quietly. "These people...they'd just as soon shoot you down."

Mr. Mustache flicked his cigarette into the gutter without breaking eye contact with Charlie. He took a step closer to Price who didn't flinch, just opened his coat a little more. The outsider muttered an obscenity, probably *fuck you*, before opening his trunk, grabbing his bag of trash and throwing it in. When he closed the lid Charlie wagged his finger.

"Why don't you take another couple of bags? Do it for Miguel." Mustache Man was about to say something but then a familiar pop went off down the street, a 9mm. He moved in a way Price had seen countless times: The outsider *was* a vet, probably from the first Gulf War. Mr. Mustache caught how Charlie had watched his reaction and the contempt in his eyes was replaced by curiosity.

"You're weird as fuck, son and I can see you've been somewhere." The outsider fished out his Parliaments and little another one, still trying to read the cop.

"I meant what I said, shit is gonna get hard," Mr. Mustache sighed. "You best get the back of your own kind," he added. He waited for a response from Charlie but when none came the outsider opened his trunk, put the trash in, and drove off.

The Lawyer

Then: Neither of them were even teenagers nor would they ever be. Price looked from their still bodies over to the fake AK-47. His minders were looking everywhere except where the dead children lay. Was it guilt? No, Charlie knew both men well enough to understand neither felt any guilt. The children had approached Price with what appeared to be a gun, his guards simply did as they were trained to do. Charlie still felt anger, though. Words were not coming, not that they would have had any effect. The smell of blood was strong; nothing could be done but keep moving.

Even earlier: On Charlie's third morning in jail the guard took the prisoner to a room he hadn't been in: Battered metal table maybe two by six surrounded by four metal chairs. Smell of Pine Sol and the ghost of cigarettes and coffee.
"Have a seat, your lawyer will be in directly."
The prisoner did as he was told and the guard left. Price sat in one of the chairs and thought about all the condemned men and women that had sat in that same chair---had the guard threatened them as well? Had he menaced them with his scowl and over-sized penis? Probably, the guard clearly had borderline psychopathic tendencies. The door was opening, bringing a stranger and new smells: Expensive cologne, boutique soap, and poor coffee in the styrofoam cup. He nodded at the prisoner and asked the guard to wait outside. The guard agreed with a compliant smile and then---behind the lawyer's back---touched the front of his pants and winked at the prisoner. The lawyer took a sip of the coffee and winced.

"Couldn't you have gotten busted somewhere with better coffee?"

The prisoner just stared at him. It was clearly a joke---was he supposed to respond or was it rhetorical?

"Relax, Charlie, I was told all about you; I have a pad and some pens if writing would be easier."

Pity; the last thing he wanted or needed.

"No, it's alright," Price replied.

The lawyer took another sip of coffee and allowed sternness into his voice. It didn't play, he was too soft looking---did that make him ineffectual fighting a case?

"It's not alright, Charlie; you carried a loaded handgun across state lines, into *Texas* of all places. How does a smart guy like you do something so stupid?"

Charlie just shrugged. It *had* been stupid and he *had* been niave: He was a white guy carrying a gun through Texas and assumed the police would be okay with it. Price had done everything right down to obeying the speed limit...it hadn't stopped the cop from pulling his rig over.

"Sorry I'm late, by the way," the lawyer added in the present. "My motel is fifty miles away and I don't dare speed, I don't want to end up in here with you."

The coffee smelled burnt. Too many people left the pot on the hotplate---was it really so hard to put it in a thermos when it finished brewing?

"No, you really don't," Price agreed.

The lawyer pulled a laptop out of his shoulder bag.

"I'm going to be honest, Charlie: You fucked up and I don't know if I can get you out of here."

The prisoner thought of the guard pushing him into the wall and felt as if he were falling through the floor. His face must have shown it because the lawyer grabbed his wrist---

Clammy skin, hair peeking out of his French cuffs; his entire body was probably covered with hair---

Charlie pulled away without thinking. The lawyer looked hurt, it flashed in his eyes for a moment.

Great. My one hope, my one link to the outside world, and I'm alienating him.

The lawyer was clearly composing himself, getting past hurt feelings; why had Price pulling away hurt him?

"There is an out, Charlie: An individual reached out to me and paid my retainer; he said that you would know who I am referring to."

Price did; the individual in question had been pursuing Charlie for a decade. In the past, he would get a letter or a call a couple of times a year. Since September 11th, 2001 the letters and calls came once a *week*. The jail was fucking with Charlie's ability to make words and say them to other people. He managed to smile at the attorney to buy time, a friendly false front until he could locate the words and get them out of his mouth.

"I don't do well with authority," Price said. "There's...no buffer, no space when you're in that situation. I couldn't hack it."

The lawyer looked up from his laptop. There was kindness in his eyes, it appeared genuine and Charlie felt guilty for pulling away. The attorney was not an attractive man despite his expensive suit and haircut, probably had been rejected a lot.

"And this is better?" He gestured around the room. "I saw the guard touching the front of his pants---how do you see that playing out, Charlie?"

The lawyer had a point.

"The man who hired you, he knows I am waiting on information..." Price began.

"News on your sister?" The other man asked. "He said you'd ask about her—how long has it been since she disappeared?"

Three weeks.

Communication coming out of Afghanistan is bad; she's probably just somewhere remote. Don't worry about it, she's probably fine.

No, his instincts told him that Celeste was in trouble.

"He told me she was writing a piece about the bombing of some statues or something," the lawyer said.

The prisoner's fear for his sister was blocking the words up again, shrouding them, cutting off their air---

No, this was important; he would force them to fall in line and do what he wanted.

"The Buddhas of the Bamiyan," Charlie said softly. "They were blown up a little over a year ago. Celeste was there to do an article on the site, local reaction, things like that."

The lawyer was consulting something on his laptop.

"Wow, Afghanistan—can she speak their language? What is it called?"

"Pashto," Price replied. "We both speak it."

"That must be why those people want you to work for them," the attorney said grimly. "Are you afraid of getting shot or something? I mean, I know you said you hate authority."

"Don't hate it, just...I don't know how to describe it."

The lawyer closed his laptop and leaned across the table. He was clearly looking to confide in Charlie or something like that.

"The individual who paid my retainer will be coming here in twenty-four hours. I guess he will be at some base nearby and decided to visit you in person. You can stay in your cell and refuse to see him if you want but I wouldn't recommend it."

The lawyer packed his computer away and stood up.

"Consider your options, Charlie, there are two of them to be exact."

I really should shake his hand. It would be a good thing right now...

But Charlie didn't want to shake the lawyer's hand; All that body hair, it was probably *everywhere*; he couldn't make his body comply. The lawyer looked sad but it was just another flash, he was a quick change with a bag of masks.

"Goodbye, I really hope things work out for you."

Charlie watched him go.

Now: The cop became aware of his surroundings; how long had he been leaning against a fence? It was chain link, waist high, corroded; guarding an abandoned house. It was a dangerous place to zone out, to just get lost in memories---

Were those real memories, though? It feels like...feels like a story I came up with for whatever reason.

But it was *vivid*, down to the smell of old urine in the cell and the way the attorney's watch had looked: Gold, not a Rolex but another pricey brand. Despite his surroundings, the cop closed his eyes and leaned against the fence again. He saw a jail cell, *his* cell, but the details had changed: The walls were stones held together with mortar and the floors were earth with dirty looking hay spread on them.

For the bodily waste, they wouldn't even give you a bucket because you're Irish.

"Irish," Charlie opened his eyes.

A couple of teenagers had been walking on the opposite sidewalk and had stopped to check Price out. The cop opened his jacket wide enough to reveal the Ruger, the kids walked on.

They treated me especially bad because I was Irish.

Charlie had carried the ugly memory of his time of a Texas jail for nearly twenty years---why did it suddenly feel fake? There had been a time in a small jail, he *knew* that, but if it wasn't Texas where had it been? Why was he seeing a jail that was clearly from a long time ago, maybe hundreds of years? The teenagers were out of sight but they would be back, his instincts told him that. Charlie walked on.

Ghosts

Price was thinking about the Glenlivit he had left on the bar. There wasn't any whiskey in the house and the craving he was feeling was the reason why. Glenlivit. Johnnie Walker Black. Even Clan McGregor. Back home, he distracted himself by going over the pants he had been wearing that morning; if the cleaner could get the blood out the tear could be easily mended. The Internet was a black hole he didn't want to get lost in so he checked the time and allowed himself a strict ten minutes. There was a news segment about someone named Low2Dipz who had been gunned down outside a motorcycle dealership. According to the story he was a 20 year old rapper; maybe he had been robbed or maybe it was a beef. How had he been shot? Had it been a head shot that killed him instantly or had it been to the torso which may have given him a few minutes or longer? There weren't any details, maybe the story was too new or maybe no one else thought it was important. Charlie closed his laptop and looked over at the piano. What would happen to the kids who had shot at him? Did they have strong parents who would keep them in line? Or, would they fall in with gangs? Would they live long enough to have good lives or be gunned down over some stupid beef or trying to prove themselves? Charlie thought of the boy with the 9mm, the anger in his eyes and the way it sounded when his arm snapped---
They had been alive when he had left the scene, he was pretty sure of that.
Am I?

But there was the vision of the two of them lying still on the cement, blood and gore fanned out behind them.

Then?

Now: Price thought of the Glenlivit, how it held the light, how it smelled. The cop reopened his laptop, checked the weather after the news, and then his ten minutes were up.

Charlie walked until he was well out of his neighborhood, walking purposefully down unfamiliar streets with their own stripped cars and people drinking in front yards who watched Price suspiciously: White guy walking alone. An Oldsmobile with big rims and bass rattling the tinted windows rolled up. Charlie unbuttoned his jacket as it came to a smooth stop two houses down. The brake lights seemed redder than normal and the clunk of the transmission going into park seemed muted. The cop didn't change his pace but kept his attention on the passenger windows. Odds were low that they'd just blast but the odds were decent that they'd try and mess with him somehow. A head leaned out out the front passenger window: Mix of Black and Hispanic. Mid-twenties. Handsome. Eyes a combination of hard and warm.

"Hey, you're that cop," the man in the car said.

Price just stared at him. Handsome Man had the driver back up so he was alongside the man on the sidewalk.

"Why didn't you shoot those kids, bro?" Handsome man asked. "They had guns."

Price studied Handsome Man. On the surface he seemed reasonable but he probably played a role in *why* those kids had shot at him.

"You just answered your own question," Charlie said.

He didn't bother concealing his animosity: Price had placed Handsome Man and knew his story. The two men just looked at each other. Handsome Man was wearing some sort of cologne that smelled like whiskey and vanilla; it was odd that he had a smell.

"Thank you," Handsome man smiled.

He touched his forehead with his left index finger as if saluting before saying something to the driver as he rolled his window up. The bass started rattling the windows again and the Oldsmobile drove off. Price walked back the way he had come.

The Groundsman

An older man was raking leaves three houses down. There was no expression on his face which Price took for inner peace or at least inner contentment. He could rake leaves; it would be peaceful and he would be alone. Maybe the money wouldn't be so good but he could give up his house and rent a room or something. It'd be worth it for some peace, whatever that was.

A Valuable Commodity

Back home, Charlie sat at the table with a glass of water in front
of him. He didn't want water, he wanted whiskey, but that made
tolerating the water and even drinking it even more important.
He closed his eyes and brought back his memories (?) of the jail in
Texas. The first one was of when the guard had left a hardcore gay
porn magazine on Price's cot. It was perfectly squared against the
lower left corner: Thought had gone into that, lots of thought.
Too much thought. The cell door closed behind the prisoner as he
stared at the magazine. The guard was chuckling a little; it was the
most humorless laugh Charlie had ever heard. *Dangerous Dongs*
was the name of the magazine: It looked rumpled and water
stained, pages appeared stuck together. What was he supposed to
do with it? He sure as fuck didn't want to touch it. If he knocked
off the cot it would still be right there on the floor---
And what if the guard took offense at his kicking it onto the dirty
floor? What if it was some kind of *present*? Charlie got four
squares of toilet paper and picked up the magazine by the cover.
It felt heavy. It probably wasn't water that had swelled the pages,
it was probably jism, lots of jism. He got the magazine up on a
shelf and let it go as quickly as possible. Why had he been carrying
the gun? No, he knew the reason, he just wasn't clear why he had
ignored the consequences.
And now he was living them.

"Fake," the cop said in the present as he opened his eyes.
How had he created such an elaborate fiction? *Why?* And then
he thought of when the kids had been killed in Afghanistan, how
he *knew* it hadn't been the first time it happened. The cop closed
his eyes again, went back to the jail in Texas.

There was nothing to write on and nothing to read but *Dangerous Dongs*.

The individual will be coming here in 24 hours.

Charlie knew what organization his benefactor belonged to; it wasn't the first or even the tenth time they had hounded him. It had all started with a battered table when he was seventeen and had been required to speak with recruiters from all four branches of the military. The words had refused to come for the Air Force. The Air Force guy had gotten disgusted and didn't bother covering it up. The man from the Navy had terrible breath as if he were dying from the inside out. Charlie had made a show of picking his nose and pretending to eat it until Halitosis Harry took the hint and left. The Marines found out about the history of discipline issues and bid Charlie good day.

And then he spoke to a Master Sergeant from the United States Army.

Yes, I saw the notes in your school file. I also see how highly you scored on your SATs and your gift for languages. Things are tense in the Middle East now, Charlie, and probably will be for a long time. It's only a matter of time before someone like you, who is already fluent in Pashto and knows some Arabic, to become invaluable.

Charlie had nodded but hadn't bothered to stop squirming in his chair. The Master Sergeant was in his face, insisting on looking in his eyes and following them if he looked away. Charlie had told the Master Sergeant that he wasn't interested but his statement had clearly been brushed aside. The moment had seemed like a victory; the words had come easily and his exit from the room without hesitation. Years later, though, Price understood that they had *allowed* him to leave the room: The Master Sergeant held the victory; Charlie Price was going nowhere.

The Irishman

Charlie got home around the time the sun was disappearing over the coastal mountains. The pile of trash on the street had grown larger. Someone had dropped off their collection of 80s porn: *Oui* and *Hustler* and *Penthouse*. It reminded him of the magazine that had been left in his jail cell; he turned his attention to the stripped car. At least it wasn't burned out, he had seen too many burned out cars in his life.

Then: Sometimes you could see or smell the flesh melted into the seats.

Now: Looking at the ruins of what had been a luxury car thinking about the boys who had shot at him; they changed from Black and wearing sneakers to Pastun and wearing sandals. What would become of those boys, the Black ones? Price wasn't worried about the smaller one, he had been terrified. For the older of them two shooting at a cop had only been the beginning of something, Charlie had seen that in the kid's eyes.

Maybe this is what it feels like to have a nervous breakdown, maybe this is *a nervous breakdown.*

Trying to center himself, Charlie sat at the piano and played a series of notes in a loop. Were the keys ivory? No, they hadn't yellowed. The plastic or whatever it was smooth, smooth as the table he had run his hand over as the Master Sergeant rolled out his spiel about everything the Army would do for---

Gilbert Franks.

He didn't see himself in a high school library, he saw himself in a bar, a *pub*. A big man in a red uniform with a pale, splotchy face and razor nicks was telling him about the benefits of joining---

"I can read your face, that is how I've made sergeant, I know people, I do," the big man took a drink from a pewter mug--*tankard?* "You're worried about the danger of a soldier's life. Understandably, but else do you have to look forward to? The Major asked us to get you out of jail. *Jail!* I know you Irish lads are known for trouble but..."

The sergeant was still letting words tumble out of his mouth but Charlie---(*Gilbert?*)---was no longer listening. Jail: He had been in jail simply for having a suspicious amount of money for a poor man, a poor *Irish* man, had foolishly left it in a bag in the shabby room he had been renting. They accused him of being a thief, jail was awful, one guard had threatened to sodomize him---

Bang! The sound of the tankard slammed onto the rough table. "You listening, Franks?" The Sergeant was leaning forward, his mouth open, his teeth were straight but deep yellow and black around the edges. "We can shove you back into jail with that pervert if you prefer!"

"No, I apologize, sergeant," Charlie/Gilbert replied. "You were saying I'd probably be stationed in Afghanistan."

Charlie was back in his living room, playing the same five notes in a loop.

I'd probably be stationed in Afghanistan.

The sergeant had a lower class British accent from somewhere in midlands like Birmingham. Whenever the dream or memory or whatever it was had to take place during when the British were fighting in Afghanistan. He got up to check his phone when the English had warred in that part of the world but then he realized or remembered when the memory dream had been set: Early 1840.

"This makes no sense," Price said to himself.

Charlie used the bathroom and then reserved a small truck on-line. Chris had asked him once why didn't just have the City pick up the trash--- the City took too long for Price's liking; his neighborhood wasn't a priority to them, something he had understood when buying the house. The realtor had been a fancy man in a well cut suit with a Porsche SUV. He had smiled when Charlie had told him the houses he was interested in but the smile had been chiseled into his face and didn't match the rest of it. Fancy Realtor had tried to talk Price out of the house---
Your credit and income will get you a house in a much better neighborhood.
He had been uncomfortable around the man with the $2000 suits and the $100000 car; the words had gone on lockdown, all windows barred and machine guns in a tower. Charlie made them emerge from behind concrete; he had known from first seeing it the house was meant to be his.

How Did He Die?

The cop had no one to talk to. Even if he had, Charlie understood that what was he was experiencing would concern a friend such as Chris:

You see, I've been time slipping. I am becoming more and more convinced that 180 years ago I was an Irishman named Gilbert Franks and that all my memories of the past twenty years have been fabricated. Oh, and I see this Gilbert Franks guy, the one who may be me from the past; he gets in my car and I can smell him.

There were no details on where Low2Dipz was shot, none of the articles Charlie found mentioned where the bullets had struck. The scene was vivid in Price's imagination, though: The rapper started to get in his luxury car as an SUV came to a stop nearby with locked brakes. Was Low2Dipz armed? Did he reach for a gun under his jacket or in his car? And then the bullets. In his mind he saw them hitting the torso and the rapper's face growing small with surprise and pain as he fell back in his car---
And then he saw the boys lying in their own blood on the dirty cement of the abandoned apartment complex. Charlie willed them to life, the little one crying as his parents lectured him. The older one in a cast and sling staring at a wall with too much anger on such a young face.

The Crush and the Kettle Drum

Price was watching crows from the kitchen when he heard a kettle drum in another part of the house. No, it was someone pounding the metal security door. That never happened; the Jehovah's Witnesses and salespeople knew better than to---

Another round from the kettle drum. One of the crows was angry about something. Charlie carried his coffee cup across the house. The gun was in the kitchen but his instincts told him that it was unneeded; people who mean you harm rarely knock. Dawn Mendez had been the one playing the kettle drum. She was wearing sunglasses and he could smell her shampoo.

"Did you *try* and find the worst neighborhood when looking for a house?" She asked.

Was it a joke or a genuine question? It was too early for thought.

"*City Pulse* says this is an *up and coming* neighborhood," Charlie said, managing a smile.

The words always came easy around her; he was pleased by that but not by what it alluded to.

"*City Pulse* is clearly full of shit," Dawn said through the slots in the metal door.

Price opened the door for her, she glanced behind him and then stepped into the house. That face: Did she smell something? You can never smell your own house's odors. The words may have come easily but a certain anxiety was shooting sparks: Was Dawn just *friendly* with him or did she see him another way? She was married but married meant different things to different people. No, having any sort of feelings for a married woman was wrong and Charlie had taken part in too many wrong things in his life. *Like shooting innocent Afghani kids in 1840 or maybe 2002 or maybe both.*

Not now, definitely not now.

"Hope I didn't derail your plans for becoming inspector," he said. She made a face and Charlie remembered that Dawn hadn't shared her plans with him; he had overheard them and made a mental note. Her expression was unreadable, there was a visible wall in front of whatever she was thinking. The words had died; for some reason they had died for both of them. Charlie realized how dark it was in the living room and opened the curtains. Dust danced in the sunlight. Mendez had started to take her sunglasses off but put them back on.

She knows. She can tell me that we saved the boys.

She could, or she could give him words that confirmed his fears. She could...and her face would change from friendliness and whatever else she felt for him into awkwardness and eventually distance.

No, he would keep his question to himself.

"Did they give you any idea how long your suspension will be?" Mendez asked.

The dust was still swirling in the sunlight. How long had it been since he had pounded the curtains? That was how you dusted curtains, right? Unhook them and take them outside and....

"No," he replied.

She had taken a step closer. What did it mean? Did he ask if she wanted coffee? Did he take a step closer in turn?

"I don't know," Price continued. "Maybe I'm not meant to be a cop."

Dawn took her sunglasses off. Her eyes were brown, he had never noticed that before. Golden brown.

"After all these years this is the first time that thought occured to you?"

She turned towards the window and the sunlight found the piece of metal on her left hand. Price took a step back, tried to exile the smell of her shampoo from his senses. Suave, it was Suave.

"No, but I am out of excuses for going back," he said, trying to keep nervousness out of his voice.

Dawn was slowly twirling her sunglasses by one of the arms---what did it mean? Every gesture, every tic means something; was she watching him as closely as he was watching her?

"I hope you change your mind," she replied.

Dawn was moving towards the door, his cue to hurry over and open it for her.

She opened it for herself but paused in between his sanctuary and the outside world.

"I saw you talking to the uniforms through the window. It looked ugly from fifty feet away."

"It was no big deal. Guys like that, they rarely do anything."

Mendez put her sunglasses on and it disappointed him.

Golden brown, I have never really seen her eyes before.

"Maybe you bring things out in people, Charlie."

The Scorpion's Tail

"Lights out!"

And then all he had was the darkness...and *Dangerous Dongs* lurking somewhere in the shadows with its pages stuck together. By the time the world was light again the prisoner would be forced to choose between two bad options.

No, fake---

There hadn't been lights in jail, when sunlight stopped coming through the openings in the stone wall it got dark until a jailer came down with a lamp. The memories of the Texas jail were eroding, morphing into a gaol somewhere in England.

Then: Charlie had thought that the visit from the Master Sergeant was the end of it. No, seventeen days later a car pulled in front of their house. It was a newer Ford Taurus, a car that didn't belong in his neighborhood, too middle America, a TV dinner on wheels. The boy watched from the window as a man in a uniform that looked like a costume got out, so many ribbons and medals. Charlie's instincts told him that Uniform Man was there to see him. Mother claimed his shoulder like a bird that smelled like sugar.

"What do you see out there, Robin?" She asked.

"I think we're about to get a visit from the military," he said through a clenched face.

Uniform saw them peeping at him from behind the curtain and smiled.

I know you spoke to Master Sergeant Lopez two weeks ago, Charlie, but I wanted to meet you in person. I'm sure you heard about the war with Iraq in Kuwait four years ago; we are preparing for further conflicts in the future in that region of the world and could really use a person with your intelligence and language skills.

His mother had protested by wringing her hands and exclaiming that her son was not going to be killed in some stupid war. Charlie had sat in silent embarrassment even if he agreed with her. Major Harrison had listened patiently but the boy caught how he was pinching the bill of the hat he had scooped off his head walking in the house—Uniform Man's smell was changing, too; he was making aggressive smells and pinching his hat even as he sat on their couch with a polite smile. That smile...Charlie could tell it hurt him to wear it as if it was a prop held onto his lips with tacks.

"If you reconsider, Mrs. Price, please accept my business card." He held out a card but she kept her hands at her side. The tension was too much so Charlie grabbed the card to end things. His mother looked at the card in his hand and then shook her head. Her hand shot out like a scorpion's tail, grabbing the card and crumpling it. Major Harrison watched the nature show with a stillness that had deadly tones to it. How many people had he killed? Vietnam, it would have been during Vietnam; he looked old enough. Major Harrison's smile grew tight as a papercut, he appeared to be staring at the hand holding his disrespected business card. There were a few moments where Charlie was certain the meeting would end in pain but those moments were killed with a burst of words from Uniform Man who then rose and left their house.

Now: Charlie was watching him leave, but he wasn't marching down a suburban walkway to a Ford Taurus, the Major---now in a red uniform---was walking out to an open carriage pulled by two black horses.

Which are the correct memories? The ones from the nineties felt like a movie he had seen and not his life. How? They had felt genuine for so long, and there are so many details: Major Harrison's office sent three letters to Charlie in the course of eleven months. Mother protested to the Army and her Congresswoman but the letters continued to creep into their mailbox. Their cousins followed Charlie to rooms and apartments he rented on his own. He got a degree in history but needed a break from school before getting his teaching credentials. Price used that time to sign on with a trucking company that paid for his behind the wheel training. Truck driving school was unpleasant, sharing a dormitory with a man with terrible body odor and overt racism, but once it was over he grew to appreciate the job; the money was decent and you were alone a lot more than he would have been as a teacher.

And another memory of a visit home after completing truck driving school:
The smell of coconut toasting, him sitting at the table in the kitchen expecting a pie. His mother brought out a shoebox and set it in front of him. Charlie recognized the box, Justin's boots, knew what was inside, and wondered why he was looking at it instead of a slice of coconut cream pie. His mother's face was the same as when she had snatched the card and crumpled it.
"I am either going to sell it or you can have it," Mother had said. The thing in the box had been a gift from a concerned aunt after a handful of break-ins across town. Not even in their neighborhood, but Auntie Gin saw the name of their town in the news and great fretful.
I don't know why you feel the need to live in a big city. But, as long as you do, I would feel better if you have this. Maybe John can learn

to shoot it; Charlie, too, when he is older. Do you still call him Robin? Robin or Charlie could learn to shoot it, as well.

His father had never bothered to take it to a range and learned to use it; the revolver was something he hadn't wanted in the first place and remained as useless as the exercise devices shrouded by dust in the garage.

"You should sell it; you'll get a few hundred, I'd guess," he had said.

She opened the box and looked inside. Her expression reminded him of the times he'd walked up to people and forced himself to talk to them. There were more words exchanged but in the end Price had left with the box...after eating a large piece of coconut cream pie with coffee.

"None of that was real," Charlie whispered to himself as he cleaned the morning dishes.

Where were the memories of his parents, then; his *real* parents?

The Bruise

Low2Dipz was an abuser, a borderline psychopath—none of the
articles Charlie read used the word *psychopath*, but it was inferred.
The young star also abused drugs, mainly marajuana but he had
developed an interest in cocaine—and then disappeared right
before his 20th birthday. It was on all the news channels; Price's
first thought was that it was a ploy for publicity. Low2Dipz
insisted it wasn't, that he had gone someplace to get his head
straight. There was a large bruise on the left side of his neck. It
was hard to see on his dark skin, but after watching the clip nine
times Charlie confirmed it was a bruise. Why was no one talking
about the bruise? It certainly looked like the result of
strangulation. No one was talking about the bruise but they were
talking about how the rapper had converted to Islam and how he
would be retiring the name Low2Dipz after the tour to promote
his current album. Digging deeper, Price found that the rapper
belonged to the mosque next to the large construction project in
another part of town. What if he had been on the verge of putting
his support behind the mosque? Would that have had an affect on
the construction project?

Quid Pro Quo

Then(?): The prisoner awoke to the sound of a club on the bars.
"Your visitor is here, Price. You gonna see him or not?"
Was he? What would it hurt to *talk* to him? Talk---if the words
would cooperate.
"Yes, sir."
The guard looked disappointed but he still opened the door to
the cage. The man with the gun was looking around for
something, probably *Dangerous Dongs*. There were others on the
block but they were silent as the two men passed. Price
understood why.

Major Harrison was sitting in the same chair the lawyer had sat in.
The difference was that, unlike the lawyer, he owned the chair.
Authority surrounded him; even the guard didn't make him
nervous. The Major's cologne was like perfumed steel, a stiletto.
Charlie recalled how it had lingered in their living room for a
couple of days after his visit.
"I don't have a lot of time, Price. I'm due in New York at six this
evening."
Now he was rushing Charlie---was it a ploy? *The decision must be
a quick one, the military...or Dangerous Dongs.*
"You don't have to talk, I know that's a thing with you. Our plan
for you is in what civilians would call Intelligence. We have a few
regions in Afghanistan where we could use you. I would want
you to go through officer candidate school. Did you get a four
year degree? I don't have your file with me."
"Yes."
The Major smiled, it almost seemed natural, not a cold thing held
in place by tacks and sheer will as before.

'

"It's a twelve week program. From what I remember of your testing back in high school it should be a breeze for you."
And here was a door away from sadistic guards and sticky magazines. What was behind the door? Dying in a foreign country? The odds were lower than the Infantry but they still existed. Price thought of Celeste and the guard shaking his penis between the bars of his cell.

What other options do I have?

The Major put his palms on the table and leaned forward. The smile left his face and in his eyes there was a serenity Charlie could not have imagined them possessing.

"I've stood naked before the fire, Price, and in the flames I saw your face."

Loving the Gun

Then(?): Sitting in his cell Charlie heard a bang that reminded him of a gunshot. It took him back to the shooting range, two days after accepting the gun from his mother. The Ruger .357 was still in the shoebox, an awkward thing to carry under one's arm as people seemed to be staring at him; they probably saw him as some weird boy man carrying a shoebox. What would happen if he loaded it wrong? He set the box on a counter and reached inside it. The chill of the metal made him think of snakes, things not to be underestimated.

Looking out the stationary target, aiming the heavy revolver... With the first shot he only glanced the white paper but he still *knew*---

The shooter understood what his mistake had been and how to correct it. The revolver felt natural in his hands, is a gun really something that should feel so natural in your grip? Charlie looked down the barrel towards the target again and took a deep breath.

Like his research into Afghanistan, mastering the Ruger became an obsession. He went to the range twice a week and found places far out in the country where he could shoot it; there had been plenty of beer cans to use for targets. Price forced himself to fire the gun without ear protection, it was painfully loud at first---
A loud crash in another part of the jail pulled him into the present. What time was it? Had to be close to midnight. After midnight it would be twenty-three days since anyone had heard from Celeste. Twenty-three days of worry and feeling helpless. If he signed on with the Army they'd send him to Afghanistan; there was no question in his mind considering he was fluent in

Pashto. He'd be in the same country as Celeste, he could find her and make sure she was safe---

Don't be an idiot: In the Army you can't just go off on your own. Also, there are months of training stateside most likely and once in Afghanistan where would I even start looking?

Logic attempting to elbow into a space Hope would die to preserve.

The Mosque

Now: Price drove aimlessly. Traffic thickened and came to a stop. He checked the clock, it was too early for rush hour. Two blocks further he saw that the construction project was the culprit, a semi with a long trailer struggling to back into the site. Women wearing hijabs were standing on the sidewalk watching the driver of the Peterbilt wrestle his steering wheel; his face was as red as his cap. Their imam joined the women. Charlie pulled into their parking lot, rehearsing what he would say to the imam. There was something, something about the Muslims and the construction site and Low2Dipz—everything felt *connected*. Hearing the car pull in the imam walked over with a tight smile, a *you had better not waste my time* smile. Price lost the words he had found and understood that trying to force them back would only push them deeper into the darkness. He also understood that asking the questions he needed to ask was important. Charlie rolled down his window and formed a hopefully friendly looking smile.
"This noise must make it hard to do services," he said.
The imam looked suspicious---was it because Price was an infidel?
"Oh, the mosque is very well built," he said. "We carry on quite well."
The imam crossed his arms and rose to his full height.
"We are not about to give up," he added. "We have worked too hard to make this a good place."
"Yes, I can see you have." Charlie said that in Arabic.
The imam made a face that could have been stern or could have been surprised. Had he said what he meant to say? His Arabic was far from perfect.
"Who are you?" The imam asked firmly, in English.

"I was curious about the mosque when I heard that Low2Dipz had joined your people."

The imam shook his head and said something in Arabic that Price didn't recognize.

"I'm sorry, my Arabic---"

"We call him Jerome," The imam said in English. "That other name, it was part of the problems we were helping him clean up."

Something moved out the corner of Price's eye, a crow that had landed on a nearby powerline. It called out once.

"I am sorry for your loss, it must have been a sad time for you."

The imam followed Charlie's gaze to the power line. The sight of the bird clearly displeased him.

"There is no reason for sorrow, Jerome's past was too big of a monster to kill."

"I understand he was starting to speak out about the construction project---"

The man in the robes took a step back but the rage coming off him easily filled the extra space.

"Who are you? I insist you answer this as an American citizen!"

Charlie looked over at the mosque and then back at the imam, every wire inside him being pulled tight.

"I'm just someone who read about Jerome's murder and am curious about it, what really happened."

Despite what the imam said about sorrow he was clearly struggling with some.

"It does not matter, the boy is dead, we move on."

It was time to go; Price wished the imam a good day and started backing out. The Muslim tapped on his hood.

"All things happen as God wills it," he said firmly.

"Understanding that is the only way to keep your head in this world."

The imam walked off. Hearing yelling in the distance, Price saw that the Peterbilt had knocked over a temporary fence. A man who may have been a supervisor was pounding the passenger door of the truck. The crow fled the line.

The Man in the Bowler

Celeste had left for the world by the time his mother's arm moved like a scorpion. Her room would never change, though; their mother wouldn't allow it. After his sister left Price would go to her room and close the door. He would lie on her bed with the door closed and take in her scents, soaps and shampoos and perfumes; the smells each of us send out through our pores unconsciously. Charlie sought all those things.

The photograph was still on her wall, the one Charlie was always drawn to when he went into his sister's room: A man from the first years of the 20th century. He wore a bowler and a large mustache. Price never asked Celeste the man's name because he already knew it and that somehow they would meet again. His sister had been so enamored by the composition of the photograph that she had spent months attempting to duplicate it with a dozen or so different subjects. Charlie had wanted to point out it was foolish because cameras had changed so much; there was that desire but it was outmatched by his love for Celeste and his automatic support for her. In the end, she got a composition she was happy with. The man in the original shot became a friend to Price, someone he could talk to and express thoughts that came smoothly and with no anxiety.

Now: A Black family had moved in next door to Price's family---why had that detail come up? They had a baby, much younger than their other children, when Charlie had been in Afghanistan. He was pretty sure the baby's name was Jerome.

Then: A White family had lived there before. They had a boy and girl close in age to the Price children. The boy had been cruel and mocked Charlie's difficulty with people. The girl and Celeste had been friends but all Prices had cut ties with the family due to the boy's insensitivity to Charlie.

Then: Coming back on leave with bad news, then worse news. Not going there. No fucking way.

Active Shooter

Now: Price walked out his back door to the desert. He had spread several yards of decomposed granite and planted cactus and mesquite trees and yuccas. Some had survived, some had not. There was a lavender bush on the edge of the yard to draw the bees in. The insects had come in and thrived and it gave Charlie a sense of pleasure he had not expected. There was no word about the suspension. Price understood that he was fortunate to still have his job whether that was a good thing or not. He closed his eyes and listened to the crunch of the rock under his shoes. Someone was watching him; a crow on the neighbor's roof.

Then: Sometime after returning home from the Army sitting in the Volvo wagon he would later destroy driving it off road when drunk. There was a bottle in his lap when he pulled in front of his childhood home, something cheap as those were the quantity over quality days. His mother was watching from the drapes almost shyly. No, she would not be shy, she would be anxious. Mother was expecting news about Celeste. Charlie had it and he wished he didn't, he wished that more than he had wished for anything.

Now: Price knew something was wrong when he saw Waving Arms Woman. He had been driving aimlessly when she had moved into his field of vision for less than a second. Waving Arms Woman was running across the parking lot of a warehouse; he pulled into the lot after spotting her. When Charlie turned off the motor he heard the popping of gunfire, an AR 15. He called the situation in and was instructed to wait. Price agreed, ended the call, and got out of the car with the Ruger drawn. Where had

Waving Arms gone? There was an oak that had to be a century old near the front doors. Price checked the branches for birds and then made his way inside.

"Fuck, there's another one!" An older woman croaked that as she cowered behind a cart with a rotund man and a woman barely out of her teens. The young woman looked over and wasn't impressed, going back to whatever she was doing on her phone.

"I'm a cop. Where is he?"

"No idea. Shots get far away and then closer," the younger woman said, not looking up from her mobile.

"He's looking for people," The rotund Guy said in the drowsy tone of someone in shock. "Kyle lost the football pool, thinks we cheated him."

"That's why that nut is shooting us?" Older Woman looked outraged.

Price was already walking away. Smelling a familiar smell he looked in a cubicle and saw a body in a pool of blood. Female, maybe forty. White. There was a poster of a Matisse painting on the wall. It was just a print but a good one. More gunshots, someone yelling---not pain yelling, panic yelling. There was someone begging to be let go and then another voice calling them a liar: *You're a fucking liar!* Those four words over and over. At some point the mantra would end and Panic Guy would be shot down by Accusing Guy. The cop ran in the general direction of the yelling and came across Panic Guy on his knees, seeing but not seeing, a dark spot on the front of his chinos spreading. Looking at him Price could see that Panic Guy was useless and kept walking. Another body in a cubicle, a live one: Male. Hispanic. Thirties. Too much cologne, it even overwhelmed the smell of his blood. Hispanic Guy looked up at Price.

"Can you help me?" He asked weakly, fear in his eyes.

"I called for help. They'll be here in a minute."

"Okay, maybe I'll rest a bit---"

"You go to sleep and you die. Got it?" Price said sharply. "Do what you have to do to stay awake, stab yourself with a pen, just stay awake, got it?"

"Okay..."

The cop walked on. The Shooter had gone through a plastic barrier into the warehouse; a big space, a lot of shelves to take cover behind and shoot from. Was he military or a civilian? An empty bottle of Corona was on a lower shelf tucked between some boxes. Wouldn't canned beer be better for secret on the job drinking? Crushed it could blend in with the soda cans. Of course, there was the smell---

The Shooter was two rows over.

The words that had come so easily with Hispanic Guy were gone. Price didn't want to talk, didn't want to interact with the Shooter; everything was a jumble in his head aside from the instinct to neutralize the Shooter.

"I'm a cop. Let's talk this out," he said clearly.

"What is there to talk about?" Kyle asked, anger in his voice, fear as well.

The shooter had a firm voice, a good voice for calling back orders, *possibly* a military voice. He had been distracted from killing Panicked Guy, though; a trained killer wouldn't have been.

"Well..." Price concentrated on forcing the mess of letters and ideas into words and thoughts and pushing them out his mouth. "Is all this about losing the football pool?"

Laughter, the laugh of a man about to fall off the edge of the world.

"Do you think I'm that fucking petty, bro? Do you think I'd be this pissed off about a football pool?"

High notes mixed in with the normal voice---mania. Price had a feel for where he needed to shoot when the moment came; his instincts told him it was inevitable. The struggle was not seeing the Shooter as a monster. No, he was just a normal guy---maybe even a good guy---that had gone somewhere no one should go. "Okay," Charlie said calmly. "Why don't you tell me what this is about?"

Had the Corona drinker been shot? What if the shooter was the Corona drinker? What if he drank to deal with his workplace?

"I see you, bro," Kyle said bitterly. "You're trying to talk me into putting my gun down, I've seen this shit on television."

"I'm just trying to keep you alive---"

"What? You think you can just shoot me? You think I'm a pussy? Fuck you!"

Price had a clear shot. He wanted to take it and hated how much the idea appealed to him. No more words were coming; his brain wanted the Shooter dead. No, he would fight it, he would find the words and keep the Shooter alive...

And then they were not alone: SWAT, two of them appearing behind Price which put him in the crossfire. Instinctively Charlie dove down as they barked at the Shooter who looked confused, like a child; he was moving his weapon without thinking and---

Shots followed by the Shooter's face becoming large with surprise and then small with pain as a dozen bullets jerked his body around. Price stood up. The Ruger was still in his firing hand; he reholstered it. The SWAT guys were approaching the shooter and saying things down their radios. Charlie couldn't make out the words as he walked out of the warehouse. His arms were up out of habit. The cop in charge walked up to him. He was so built up it appeared that he didn't have a neck.

"I thought they told you to wait for backup, Inspector."

"I had to take action, Sergeant."

The Sergeant was studying Price's face, staring in his eyes. Price hated it but he wasn't going to be the first one to look away.

"I was talking to the guy," Charlie said. "I could have talked him down."

Did he believe that? Not really.

"We had to terminate him," the Sergeant said in a flat tone. "Shooter had a history of mental illness; he was a sick dog that had to be put down."

Price shook his head in disgust and walked away.

"We're going to need to get your information, Inspector."

"Text me."

Those two words were all he had. Price retraced his steps and found the Hispanic guy.

"Still awake," he sighed, a Bic disposable pen was in his right hand. "Fucking hurts," the wounded man added.

"Yeah, it will..."

"Ambulance coming?"

"The cops had to make sure it was safe but they're probably just outside."

Seeing how much the Hispanic guy was hurting was a positive sign; he was alive, he wasn't slipping into the darkness.

"They kill him?" The wounded man asked.

"Yeah."

There was no joy on the wounded man's face, not even relief.

"Guess it was going to happen," he said before the pain overwhelmed him again.

"Yeah."

The paramedics were in the building. Charlie waved at them and they started walking down the aisle.

"Help is here. Take care."

Price walked off without waiting for a response.

Loud Neighbor

He had walked away from the wounded man but the ordeal was far from over. There were questions to answer with words as eyes locked with his and would not release.

Then(?): Visiting home a few years earlier with good news: He had made Inspector. His father had been home then and both parents were happy for him but he could also see surprise in their eyes---how had he done it considering his condition? In his memory, Price could see the meal of turkey breast and salad that his mother had thrown together. Was there a celebratory drink? No, that had been after he had stopped. More details of the conversation were coming, his father complaining about the boy next door playing hip-hop loudly. Price offered to go next door in an official capacity to speak to the teenager. His father had winced and reminded his son that the neighbors were Black and such an action might be seen as insensitive. The neighbor was a good kid, they would give him another week before knocking on the door themselves. A name had been mentioned; Price was almost certain it was Jerome.

Black Charger

Price sat in his house thinking about whiskey, recalling how the Glenlivit had looked when he swirled it in a heavy glass. He was drinking water and was determined to drink only water until he went to sleep. There were pops off in the distance, small caliber, maybe a .22 Beretta. He thought of the boys that had chased him and contemplated whiskey again---

The air had changed—someone was out front watching the house. Price grabbed the Ruger off the top of the spinet and walked out the back door. Two scents dominated: Cut grass and an acrid smell that may have been meth. Peering through a knot hole in the side yard fence he saw a black Dodge Charger. Stock rims, not a local. Plates were not visible. He unlocked the gate and walked out front towards the car. It started up and slowly drove off; Charlie understood who had been watching him.

Gilbert Franks

Then: They knew that he had been to the North. Loyalty had been an illusion, those who had spoken in quiet voices that they understood and "had his back." It had been a mistake to trust them and now he was on his way to the Major's office.

Now: It took effort not to fixate on the coffee stain. How could a man be so absorbed with some details and miss others?

"I am a hundred percent on your side in this case, Price," the Captain said. "Going in was the right call, you may have saved lives."

Charlie looked up from the stain. A normal man would not be fixated on discolored carpet, a normal man would be meeting his boss's gaze with a slight nod and smile, possibly a "thank you" for seeing his side in the warehouse shooting. The words were in hiding, though. After a few moments he managed the smile and nod.

"We want you back, Price, but you're going to have your work cut out for you."

"I understand."

Why had he said that? Those words indicated that he was fully committed to being a cop again. Was he?

The smell of Axe body spray gave way to the smell of the secretary's perfume---it was surprisingly expensive smelling for such a plain woman---and then industrial cleaners in the hallway. The hall was empty and the lighting was poor. Was it always like that or was it his mind playing tricks? The smell of lavender, a presence approaching from behind.

"Come with me to the morgue."

He turned to face a man whose mustache was tilted by a knowing smile. Price didn't ask questions: If Gilbert Franks thought they should go to the morgue there was a good reason. There was a world of elegance and civility, of thought and wit, and Gilbert Franks was a glimpse of that particular something that had passed. It was now a dot long in the distance, a forgotten time.

Charlie drove them cross town to the new hospital. Gilbert sat silent in the passenger seat with his hands primly in his lap.
"We're lucky, Charlie--you know that, right?"
"What makes you say that?"
"We have nothing to lose."
A young woman was sprawled next to a Plaid Pantry. She was awake but appeared strung out.
We're lucky...we have nothing to lose.
Price thought of Celeste and wasn't sure he agreed; maybe everything we've lost is enough, those things that weigh us the remainder of our lives—the price of existence. The young woman was growing smaller in the rear view mirror. Should he turn around and see if she needed help? Maybe he could help her that day but what about tomorrow? She was as pale as a ghost in a world that could no longer see her.

The hospital would have fit in the Soviet Union, a gray monolith with dirty looking windows. Price parked next to a purple Chrysler with a Low2Dipz memorial in the back window. He tried to remember a boy named Jerome before the ugliness bloomed inside him; there weren't enough memories of his neighbor to make it happen and who knew if any memories he pulled up would be real. Gilbert chatted about the design of the building and the choice of floor tile.
We have nothing to lose.

Price saw a stained chair in a waiting area and made a face. Maybe it was coffee, maybe it was something else. Franks opened an unmarked door to a stairway leading downstairs. The morgue tech appeared East Indian and had too large of a mustache for his body. It was surprisingly full considering the youthfulness of his face. He nodded at Charlie and ignored Gilbert, it wasn't his fault. Price offered his identity and a name and was led to a drawer. The morgue tech left the room. There was a gunman from the warehouse under a sheet, his face was set forever in anger and pain.

"Tell me about truck driving, Price," Franks said.

The question was so out of nowhere the words hadn't the time to get bottled up.

"I drove trucks a long time ago."

Gilbert slid the sheet back over the dead man.

"Before Afghanistan?"

Had Low2Dipz been in this morgue? In this same drawer? Now the memories of Jerome were coming back; it was possible that they were created as his interaction with the boy had been less than minimal---how could there be so many genuine memories?

"Before Afghanistan. Why are you asking?"

Then: Sitting on Celeste's bed, looking at a picture that had helped her become and photojournalist, go to Afghanistan, and---

Now: "Why did you quit it to join the Army and go to Afghanistan."

Charlie was going in and out of the morgue, quick cuts to a photo of Celeste that was still in his parents' living room. The last photo of her. The Army had one more but Price couldn't go there.

"You know this is right, however frustrating it may be---"

Gilbert's voice, coming from next to him, coming from a photograph.

"I can do this job," Charlie said. "I know it, but they keep stopping me…"
The words, even as they passed his lips, had a petulant taste to them.
"That's ego talking, Price, *pride*, I know you see it."
Maybe. No, *probably*.

And then he was sitting in his car alone remembering the day Dawn Mendez had played the kettle drum and how her eyes were golden brown.
Then: A beige gully. A world of dust. A man in a tunic and knock off Levis half talking to Price and half yelling down his phone in Pasto. There were thorn bushes everywhere---how was the man in the tunic wearing flip flops? How did they not fall apart in the rough terrain? And they came to a shape---

Now: America. A city, looking across the street at a Jack in the Box---it could still be dangerous to go back, back *there…those* memories. Days and weeks and months of amber liquid and lost time and deep hurt both mental and physical.

Then: A shape. A woman. She had been dead a few days. It was remarkable no scavengers had gotten to her but the heat had. A medic moved into frame---Beatty, that was his name; he was always clearing his throat and spitting and argued one time with Price about music. Beatty and one of the others wrestled the body into a zippered bag. Charlie wanted to fight them: *She can't breathe in there.* It was the most ridiculous thought he had ever had. He couldn't smell her shampoo, just decay and other smells that had no business coming from someone so beautiful and young. Celeste had died of a shot to the lower abdomen; that was all Price heard before shutting down. Gut shot. Sometimes you lived in days for agony---

No, not necessarily; maybe the bullet hit the vena cava and she bled out quickly--

He would tell himself that but the monster had a louder voice: *You know she suffered. They gut shot her and fucked her as she slowly died in great pain. Dirty men, cruel men who would have been rough with her as she needed comfort more than anytime in her life.*

Now: Sitting in his car in America. The sound of construction in the distance. The city was changing, the world had moved on. In the office of the magazine Celeste worked in there were no *in memoriam* pictures of her. It had been nearly two decades, the odds were low that any of the people working there had heard the name Celeste Price.

Then: The Afghanis and Pakistanis who had done that to his sister---five men---were all dead. Price had remained sober long enough to ensure that. And then he could drink and live every cliche a man in deep grief will go through including landing in the brig. There was no sadistic guard, no copy of *Dangerous Dongs* with the pages stuck together, just a hangover made more savage by a malfunctioning air conditioner.

So...you managed to kill the men who abducted, raped, and murder you sister? I hope you understand your actions are meaningless, Price; they were paid to take the actions they took by an American. He scripted every detail.

Major Harrison had told him that. Someone had paid locals to kill his sister and make it look as if it were the act of *terrorists*. By the time Price had recovered and gotten out Harrison had been killed in a helicopter crash. It was over, Price would get no more information to back up what the Major had told him.

Now: No, it was not over. It would never be over until he came to the end of a trail. At the end of the trail there would be a beautiful clearing and a man whose name he did not yet know. The man would turn, Charlie would see his face, and then he would shoot him in exactly the same place Celeste would have been shot. There would be no rape, but there would be agony and Price would watch every moment of it and let the sharpness of those seconds and minutes and hours cut away the memory of watching one of the few people he had ever loved zipped into a fucking bag.

Ghosts, Part Two

A plastic bag with nine Corona bottles had been added to the pile of garbage on Price's street. An empty pack of Russian cigarettes had been set on top of the stripped car. The way it was aligned with the edge of the roof made it appear *placed*. Charlie grabbed the pack, took it into his house, and set it on top of the spinet. What had drawn him to them?

Then: Ivan---a loud man in his late fifties with missing teeth you could see when he laughed. Had they been knocked out or had they fallen out? Price had never asked. Ivan would tell stories about his time in the Russian Army in the 80s. Most of the stories would end with meeting a woman and staying in Afghanistan after the other Russians left. It was Ivan who had helped him find Celeste.

Now: Many years later Price was staring at a package of cigarettes on top of a piano.

He hit a note then another, B and then Gb. It was time for a walk.

Price took the bus across town. It was only eight, maybe too early for any action. Each block was worse than the one that had preceded it. He got off at a stop in front of a bar called the Downstroke. The purple paint was flaking off and the smell of urine was strong. Price headed down a sidestreet thinking about the day they had found Celeste. It was the worst thing he could think about, so bad it incompassitated him. He pushed the thought away. A car was rolling up behind him, slowing, checking him out...the way the music was coming told Price a window had come down. He reached into his jacket and laid a hand on his holster. The car came to a stop next to him. Charlie recognized the engine and relaxed some.

"Are you trying to get shot?" The handsome guy from the other night said. "Why do we always find you where no white guy should be walking alone?"

Price had no answer to that.

"Bro has a .357," someone laughed inside the car. "That's some old school shit right there."

His friends laughed, all but the handsome guy. The handsome guy looked troubled.

"You suicidal or something?"

Price wanted to ask why he'd care but the question felt wrong. The man in the car realized he wasn't going to get an answer and motioned to the driver. The Oldsmobile drove off, Price could smell marijuana smoke coming out of the windows and saw that the plates had expired nine years in the past. He turned around and walked back the way he had come.

Pin Ups

There were bones and dried blood next to the Buddhist temple.
Price couched down to determine what sort of animal had once
held the bones in its body. After a few moments, he concluded
that they had belonged to a pig. A raspy looking couple were
arguing next to a travel trailer. The trailer appeared ancient,
maybe from the mid-sixties. Once it had been a casual thing,
something a family with extra money had bought for vacations.
Now it was a home to a couple of cranky tweakers.
We're lucky...we have nothing left to lose. Gilbert had said that.
Then: Sitting on the edge of Celeste's bed, searching for guidance,
searching for a teacher.

A man in plaid pants was rummaging in a shopping cart in front
of the Fat Chance. He was singing "That Girl" off key---what had
happened to Stevie Wonder? How could someone create such
amazing music in the 70s and then just dry out? There was a dark
stain on the inside of one of the legs of the plaid pants; Charlie
wanted to believe it was coffee. Walking in the bar he could smell
that someone had smoked meth in the bathroom again. Chris had
a tension to him when he saw his friend walk in that Price felt
obligated to relieve.
"I'm going to ignore what I'm smelling this time," Charlie said.
The bartender's expression changed from worry to curiosity.
"Do you really care? I mean, do you care if strangers want to
poison themselves?"
It wasn't a fair question but it was still a reasonable one.
"I've been thinking about Celeste today."
Chris' expression changed a second time from curiosity to
concern.

"That either means you're drinking or that having a drink is the last thing you should do."

Price had taken a picture of the cigarette packet. He brought up the picture and slid his phone across the bar. Chris' expression changed for a third time and he muttered something in Russian that Price could almost understand.

"Ivan's? Yeah, same brand."

A regular was pounding his pint glass on the bar. The beat reminded Price of a song and he turned it over in his head to try and figure out what it was. Chris walked down the bar. The Black Vet had been playing Ms. Pac Man. He died for the last time and wandered over to take the stool next to Price. The Vet looked dazed and smelled like gardenias---perfume; he had been very close to a woman in the last couple of hours, a woman from another generation.

"Hey, man--how many people did you kill?" Black Vet asked Price.

The question set bugs loose beneath Charlie's skin. He got up from his stool and walked out of the bar. Anywhere, direction didn't matter. Two blocks down the street his phone beeped: A text from Chris.

"What the fuck did LeRoy say to you?"

Was LeRoy the barfly's actual name or a racial epithet? It was impossible to know with Chris.

"It doesn't matter. I was starting to want a drink anyway."

Chris responded with a winky emoji. The conversation was over.

Several hours died and were swept into the past. Price still needed to talk to his friend.

Hey, man--how many people did you kill?

With the passage of several hours that had just become another eight words.

Then: Two dead black boys in an apartment complex, arranged in pools of blood. One's blood sprayed all over the number "5" on an apartment door. No, Charlie saw them playing in the vacant lot where they had fired their guns at him. Happy faces, childlike faces. It was a good thought but was it real or was it what he had to see?

Now: Where did the regulars go after closing time? Most of them seemed to be at the Fat Chance from the moment Chris unlocked the front door. Did they sleep in alleys or abandon cars? Did they have homes to go with angry partners waiting for them? The bar was locked up and the sign switched off; it was barely after two but there was no sign of the bar flies, none lingering on the street; it was as if they vanished and materialized whenever Chris turned the sign back on. Charlie sent the bar owner a text and a couple of minutes later was instructed to go to the back door. Chris was smoking a Camel and admiring a spider web on a light fixture.

"I swear, this guy has been here since I opened the place."

It seemed impossible but the cop said nothing. The bartender caught the doubt on his face, though, and appeared---

Frustrated? Frustration was something they had in common. They walked into what served as the supply room. There was a card table where Chris took his meals when the bar was closed. A closet served as his bedroom; Charlie had seen it once: It smelled of dirty sheets and an ancient *Penthouse* had lain on the floor.

"I'm worried about you, Inspector."

Price shrugged. He thought about sitting at the card table but remained standing.

"Don't."

Chris had walked into the small kitchen to get a disposable meal from the microwave, a small cardboard container with what could pass for food steaming inside.

"You haven't mentioned Celeste in years."

As comfortable as he was around Chris, Price didn't have words for that; his sister's name jumbled up all the consonants and vowels.

"We're civilians again and I'm still looking after you, Captain," the bartender said, and then burned his mouth on his food.

Charlie grunted, it was all he had at the moment. Chris was looking at a far wall moving food into his mouth but not seeming involved in eating.

"Sometimes *I* need to talk about it, man," the bartender said softly.

Why? It wasn't *his* sister and Celeste wasn't the first civilian he had seen killed. A moment of resentment and then the understanding that underneath it all his friend was sensitive. Was he? No. Price knew he had his moments but all in all he was strong. There were no other acceptable options until his calling was fulfilled.

"What do you need to talk about, about Celeste?" Price asked.

Chris made a face as if he realized what he had been eating.

"The whole thing was just wrong; a lot of shit that went down over there was wrong but what happened to Celeste sticks with me."

There was an old poster on the far wall of a Japanese model in a swimsuit. Price looked at the suit and her hair and tried to figure out what decade it was from---

What happened to Celeste sticks with me.

What was the right response to that? Did he really want Chris to elaborate?

"Everyone liked her. She wasn't awkward, she was just smart and funny and made people comfortable," Charlie said.

Chris looked at his friend intently.

"And she was brave, right?"

Maybe the eighties, the hair on the model reminded Price of the eighties.

"Yeah. We were both fascinated by Afghanistan but she was the one who went over."

Chris' face changed, it was the expression he had when expressing guilt or remorse.

"Fuck it, man," he said quietly. "Rehashing this shit is a bad idea." He started to pick up his fork and then let it fall back in the container. Chris was thinking about Celeste, Price could see it in his face and how he looked up at him and then quickly averted his eyes.

Everyone liked her. She wasn't awkward, she was just smart and funny and made people comfortable.

Yes.

"The black Charger was in front of my house again," Charlie said. He saw that Chris was looking over at the poster of the Japanese model. Her nipples were visible through the swimsuit----how many times had his friend jerked off to it. Maybe she had a name and they had conversations.

"I know why you're still looking but..." Chris trailed off.

But it won't bring her back. Perhaps, but sometimes people need to pay for what they did.

"There's no stopping now, man," the bartender added. "I get that, just stay alive, okay? Alive and sane."

Price shrugged, there weren't any words.

The Therapist

Price went home; even though it was late he did not sleep. They had scheduled an appointment with a therapist for nine the following morning. He or she would be asking about the situation with the boys shooting at him---Price was unclear on how it had ended and understood that would be a problem. He went to the piano and picked out a couple of notes, playing them over and over like a mantra, but it failed to center him or bring him peace. What was the story with the spinet? Price imagined it had been bought in the late fifties for a child to learn on. In his mind he saw a boy, a boy reluctantly sitting on the bench and stumbling through simple tunes. Eventually his parents saw it as a dead end and set him free to play ball with his friends. The boy grew up; Charlie imagined him being sent off to fight in Vietnam---

Drafted? He wasn't sure. Maybe he volunteered because someone he was close to had died over there. No, he volunteered because someone he was close to had *disappeared* over there. And that boy at the piano had found that person's body,

he had been taken to it...

Price closed his eyes and stopped playing. The visit to the therapist was going to be a problem.

At some point Price lay on the bed with his clothes on and sleep found him; mercifully there weren't any dreams. His phone sent pulses into his wall of sleep. Price showered, shaved, and put on clean clothes. The sky was overcast but he could hear the crows outside. A tricked out Japanese sedan that had been painted the color of lilacs scraped down the street, a bass signature rattling the metal. Charlie struggled with his tie—what had happened to

Piano Boy after finding his loved one in Vietnam? Had he been killed in battle? No, Price imagined him surviving the war and yet not surviving it; wounded and seeking vengeance for the loved one that had been killed.

No, the loved one that had been *murdered*...they call it *friendly fire*; sometimes it's on accident, sometimes it is clearly on purpose.

The therapist's office was in a part of the precinct Price hadn't explored, up a staircase he hadn't noticed before. The windows looked out at the sky but no trees. Charlie watched for birds but none flew by. How many hours of sleep had he gotten? An older woman in a light purple pantsuit walked into the waiting room. She was trying to look open and kind but there was something else there---

Had she been a classmate of Piano Boy? Purple Pantsuit was watching Charlie very closely; Price was skilled at throwing up walls and mazes but it was clear that she was a master with the sledge. He imagined her in the cockpit of one of those cranes that controls a wrecking ball with a warm but determined look on her face. She asked if he owned the name she sought. He confirmed that he did and they went into a room that was barely two meters square: Bookcase full of psych texts. Chair for guests. Cluttered desk. How could she work with all that clutter? Price had to look away. The bookshelf was even worse, the edges of the books were uneven and seemed to have been put there without any thought to categorization or order.

She was younger than Piano Boy...a Sophomore when he was a Senior. Had a crush on him, cried when she found out that he joined up---

Stop that. Immediately.

"There's nothing to worry about," the psychiatrist smiled. "This is just a quick chat to establish where you're at and if you feel comfortable being back on active duty."

Was he supposed to say something or would smiling and nodding suffice? Price smiled and nodded and that appeared to be enough. "So....the report says you took the action you took to save the two armed boys---is that correct?"

"Yes."

Then: Just an empty corridor in the abandoned complex. No boys in the vacant lot either, no clues as to whether they lived or died.

Now: The therapist had been watching him and was now making a face. Price couldn't determine what the face meant and it bothered him. And then the face was gone and replaced by another one. She had probably caught on to his anxiety about her previous face and had changed her expression. That just brought his anxiety back: The therapist was good at her job and that was bad.

"Your records show that you served in Afghanistan. Is that correct?"

"Yes."

She was looking at his face intently, watching every muscle and every movement of his pupils. It was nearly too uncomfortable to bear but Price understood that he had to tough it out.

"Why did you join the military, Charlie?"

He told a well prepared story about patriotism and it felt as if someone had pulled a string in his back. The shrink wasn't buying it.

"Your sister Celeste was a photojournalist there, wasn't she? Covered the Taliban and how they had destroyed those Buddhist statues, right?"

"Yeah..." That answer was immediate, but it felt wrong---a lie.

Why did it feel like a lie? The therapist was watching him, he pushed the feelings down.

"That was early 2001, wasn't it?"

No, of course it wasn't a lie: Celeste *had* gone to Afghanistan. She *had* died; he had seen her body.

"March," he answered.

"And then she disappeared?"

What if he just got up and walked out? What would they do?

You will never be reinstated. They will understand how things are and be very kind about it but you will not get your badge back. You can do this. Just sit there, keep your face blank, and answer their stupid questions.

"Yeah."

Something in the therapist's face changed, another unreadable expression: Kindness? Possibly. Concern? That would be bad. Pity? That would be even worse.

"I'm not going to ask you to relive something that is clearly uncomfortable, Inspector Price. I know you found Celeste's body, I understand how that must have affected you."

She trailed off meaningfully and smiled. Price hated the smile.

"A bit, yeah. Life...what can you do?" He replied.

Just a machine, spitting out whatever words he could pull from the mess that seemed like they'd play nicely in the conversation. The therapist was writing something on a tablet. Writing *a lot* of something.

"I am going to give you a referral if you want it. Someone not attached with the department. This is not a requirement for reinstatement, just a referral for someone to talk to if you want it."

"But...you will recommend something; what are you recommending?"

"To your Captain? That you be put back on duty. From what I have read in your file, Inspector, we need you back on the team if you feel coming back is something you really want."

She was looking at him, really looking at him. Part of him wanted to scratch at all the bugs he was feeling under his skin but another part enjoyed having someone else *see* him.

"This isn't going to go away and it isn't going to fix itself, Inspector Price. Do you understand that?"

"Yeah." But he could control it. He was strong, stronger than the memories, stronger than *Them*. The Therapist smiled, it seemed genuine and kind.

"Thank you for coming in, Inspector Price."

A Beige Wasteland

The referral therapist's office was located across town in a neighborhood Charlie was not familiar with, a beige world of newer housing tracts and shopping centers with box stores that smelled like plastic and soap. The building he sought was a discreet three story rectangular painted in two shades of beige. The trees surrounding it were small and weak, on stakes; too juvenile to provide shade. The cop parked on the edge of the lot and walked to reception. The girl behind the desk looked high school age with her hair in chestnut colored ponytails. She stared into her phone until he was breathing on her. The girl looked so annoyed the words Charlie had been practicing drifted off like balloons until he was able to grab their strings. The cop filled out the forms on a clipboard and then waited for ten minutes until a Black woman somewhere around 40 and wearing a dark blue jacket and matching skirt opened the door and smiled at him. "Charlie Price, you ready?"

He just nodded. The woman was familiar but he couldn't place it and that bothered him. She was watching him very closely—it wasn't how a therapist studies you, it was---

The interrogators. It was like how the interrogators in the Army would bore into you with their eyes. She motioned for him to sit on the couch and she sat in a simple chair facing him. He found her attractive, it was more than her looks which were more pleasant than pleasing, it was the power she gave off. Charisma.

"You seem to recognize me," she said.

"I do, but I don't know why." The words came easy, he felt comfortable around her even if he couldn't remember who she was to him.

The therapist consulted the tablet on her lap.

"Why do you think you're here, Charlie Price?"

It wasn't just a simple question, there was a question beneath the question on the surface—he could *feel* it.

"Because I didn't follow procedure by calling a fellow officer to the scene without requesting backup."

"That situation was very stressful to you, wasn't it?"

Was it a trap? It seemed like the wrong answer would keep him suspended or possibly expelled from the force.

"There is no wrong answer, we know it was," she added. "You've been having dreams that don't make sense, right?"

"That don't make sense?"

"Dreams of the past," the therapist was no longer smiling, she was watching him even more closely.

"Those kids," Charlie explained. "I've been in situations like that back in Afghanistan, I couldn't save *those* kids...so, yes, I guess my fear that I couldn't save the kids in that apartment building was stressful."

She looked down on her tablet again but it wasn't to pull up information---

She's hiding her eyes, she thinks or knows that I can read them.

The therapist looked up sharply, her smile thinner.

"What is your birthday, Charlie?"

"December 3, 1979."

Her gaze was unbroken, she paused a few seconds before speaking again.

"That was the day Charlie Price was born?"

What was she getting at? He meant to read her eyes but the therapist(?) had looked down again.

"Yes," he said, suddenly unsure.

She looked up again with a warm smile. He was curious what it meant but the words had left him. Before he could find them again she moved on to more normal questions about his moods

,

96

and whether or not he had been suffering from PTSD. She also asked him to walk her through the warehouse shooting he had tried to prevent. As he wrapped up his side of the story, there was a bell like an egg timer: Ding.

"Okay, Charlie. Can you come back at the same time tomorrow?"

"If the department is okay with it."

"They will be."

The traffic back to his side of town was intense: Had there always been so many cars on the road? Why did everyone feel the need to be so aggressive? Why was his therapist familiar? After a few minutes, the murderous traffic and the honking SUVs was unbearable, the cop pulled into a strip mall that was mostly weed choked asphalt and faded for least signs in boarded up windows.

"Pull it together," he said to himself. "You're okay just...pull it together."

After five minutes he was able to get back on the road and make his way home.

Visions

His dreams were vivid: The court of some Asian noble, Chinese by appearance. Sometime in the mid nineteenth century. Four guards on simple uniforms, muskets braced across their chests. A man Charlie knew was the emperor sitting on a dark throne carved out of dark wood---teak? Would they be using teak in China? It looked like teak. The Emperor appeared old, it wasn't just his white goatee, he seemed tired and worn out and his color was faded looking. Paper colored skin. Behind the Emperor's throne was a Black woman in a kimono. Every so often, the Emperor would look over at her and she'd whisper something in his ear. After the second time of doing that she looked directly at Charlie and smiled at him.

Would taking the light rail be more bearable? It was worth a shot even if he dreaded the smells and closeness of people. It was an hour and ten minutes to the therapist's office by train. He had to walk three blocks along a narrow sidewalk that skirted a speedway. The air was thick with exhaust and litter was all over the dying grass between the sidewalk and the parking lots of the malls and gas stations. In the waiting room, he sat in a beige chair and studied the four still life paints on the walls: A lighthouse watching a calm sea. A meadow full of blue flowers. Seagulls in flight. Mount Fuji. Ten minutes before his therapist came to get him. This time her two piece suit was dark green, it looked like silk.
"You don't mess around with your phone in waiting rooms, do you?" She observed after he took his seat on the couch.
The question caught him flat footed, he had no idea where she was going—

"You remember a time before mobile phones, don't you?" The woman in the suit continued.

"Yeah, I mean...I was almost twenty before they became common."

She nodded and noted something on her tablet.

"Why did you join the Army, Charlie?"

That question again? Maybe the new therapist hadn't gotten the notes from the previous one. He contemplated lying but could tell she would see through it.

"My sister was missing, she was a journalist over there, I wanted to join up and save her."

"So, you joined the Army." The therapist was looking into her tablet, it felt like she was evading him. No, she *was* evading him.

"My mother was angry, but she also wanted me to find my sister." As with before the answer felt wrong, like lines in a script, fiction, but it was the only answer he had.

"Between the time of your sister going missing and your joining up and everything that goes with that, how long passed?"

"I don't know...."

"It's okay, Charlie, none of this is going to affect your job. I'm trying to help you, really. Charlie, between your sister going missing and your being in Afghanistan only three weeks passed."

Three weeks? How could that be possible? It had to take longer than that to process his paperwork, another three weeks to get him through the enlistment process, it should have taken him *months* to get to Afghanistan.

"Charlie, it only took three weeks because you have connections most normal men in their early twenties do not have. And it wasn't your sister that disappeared."

How—it made no sense initially because after a few seconds there was the understanding that what the therapist was telling him was not a lie.

"Who was it, then? I remember her, the way she smiled, the smell of her shampoo...she was real."

Another pause of a few seconds.

She's milking this, I think she enjoys keeping me in suspense.

"Yes, she was real," the therapist continued. "She was the daughter of the people you were renting a room from. You felt a connection to her which is why you tried to save her and when they found her body why you just...retreated."

"Retreated? From what?"

Something bad, isn't it clear? You don't want to know, seriously---just walk out of the room.

"From who you really are," the therapist said, sitting forward.

Price just looked at her, trying to read her face, her eyes—

The truth is in there somewhere.

The bell dinged.

"You can't leave me with this question."

"Our time is up, Charlie. Come back tomorrow."

He just sat there; maybe if he didn't get up the therapist would eventually give and tell the rest of the story.

"Charlie...these things are done a certain way, at a certain pace; please trust the process, trust *me.*"

Understanding that the woman in the green suit wasn't going to bend and certainly wasn't going to break, the cop nodded and walked out of her office.

Price didn't notice the perilous sidewalk or the crowded train.

She wasn't your sister.

Then why had he been convinced that the young woman had been his sister for twenty years?

You have connections most normal men in their twenties do not have.

How? Charlie ran every bit of information about his family in his head and came up with nothing, utterly nothing.

The cop did not think he would be able to sleep but eventually it found him. In the dream he was out in the desert, a place that was mostly dark gravel with a handful of stunted trees and bushes. He had parked the Mercedes next to an old Ford Econoline. A much older man, surprisingly pale for being in the desert, was smoking a cigarette and squinting at him.

"Your time again?" The old man asked.

The question was odd but only for a moment; yes, it *was* his time again.

"We could make you Charlie Price if you want; I know you like the name and it has been long enough."

Charlie just nodded, understanding what was going on as some memories came back: A new identity, and not the first time this old man had helped him and far from the first time.

"Thought so," the old man grunted, taking the stub from his mouth and pinching it between his fingers.

Max, the old man's name was Max. He moved around the country following the good weather. Now he traveled in a 1973 Ford Econoline—

Not so long ago it had been a small wagon drawn by a brown horse with a white spot on its hip.

Max went into the side of his van and came back with a driver's license, social security card, and passport.

"Congratulations, you are now Charlie Price born December 3, 1979 in Sacramento, California, USA."

Charlie walked over and grabbed the documents.

"Thank you."

"Ah," the old man held up hand. "Hey, tell me this, Charlie Price—do you ever think about Ireland?"

Before he could ask for clarification, Charlie woke up.

Who You Are

It was still dark. The cop walked to the kitchen and started coffee.
Charlie Price had not been the name he had been given at birth,
so...what had his name been originally? And why did it feel like he
had met up with Max maybe twenty times before the scene he
had dreamt of? Why was the image of the brown horse with
white spot so vivid?
Do you ever think about Ireland?
First thought: I do not remember traveling to Ireland.
Second thought: That was because I traveled *from* Ireland.
He took a cup of coffee to the living room and sat at the piano,
picking out a few notes then chords without thinking about it.
Sometime was coming back, he could feel it like a wave rolling
into a dark beach. His concern was that it was big, he could feel
how big it was, and feared it would overwhelm him, swamp him
like a ship too small for a furious sea.

As with the previous day, Charlie did not notice the crowds on
the train or the exhaust and peril of the sidewalk. He was Charlie
Price but he wasn't, he was an Irishman and yet he had a west
coast of the US accent. It made no sense.
"If I am not Charlie Price, who am I?" He asked the therapist. "I
was so sure of my memories of my sister leaving for Afghanistan,
of my mother crying over it—"
"Charlie, your mother died nearly 400 years ago."
She said that...right? No...how could she? It made no sense. But it
did, and not knowing *why* it made sense...

The therapist reached over and touched his knee; it calmed him. Anne, her name was Anne. He knew her from China, the memory of why he had been in China was unclear but that was where he knew her from.

"And I'm Irish...." Softly, almost like he was speaking to himself.

"You haven't been Irish for a long time."

"How long?"

She pulled her hand off his knee and looked at him with a kind smile.

"We'll get to that—"

"You said my mother has been dead almost 400 years...so...I was born 400 years ago? I don't know how..."

The words left him. He *did* know how, the information was simply buried.

"You were born in 1603, Charlie."

"1603...so I'm...really old."

"If a doctor examined you he would place you around forty years old."

"It doesn't make sense..."

"Have you heard of progeria?"

"No..."

"Sad disease, ages kids rapidly; they're old by their late teens. We have an extraordinarily rare—roughly one out of eighty million people rare---genetic condition."

"So...we all age like a year every twenty---" Charlie started then stopped abruptly.

Wait...we?

Anne caught this.

"I had to replace your regular therapist because we can't be exposed."

Charlie leaned forward.

This is not real. It is not real...how could this be real? I'm not dreaming...she must be some kind of lunatic...

No, this is real...I know it is as real as the fact I have two hands and two feet.

"Because scientists and doctors would chop us up?" Words, just coming out of his mouth,

She smiled at him, it appeared genuine.

"Something like that."

It appears genuine but she has walls up, doesn't want me to know things.

"Why are you helping me?" He asked.

"Because we need you, Charlie. We need you and we can give you what you want: Revenge. You want the man who is ultimately responsible for the young woman's death but he is valuable to us. If you would take his place in our organization you could have your revenge."

He started to ask *what organization* but it had come back to him: The Foundation.

He knew the name and had the feeling they had been trying to get him to join them and that he had good reasons for not doing so.

"Think about it, Charlie. We could help each other."

He just nodded, things were coming back, things that his memory had been hiding for nearly twenty years. He had killed his mother, killed her by breaking her heart after he left their village without a goodbye because—

I was still a teenager but I had been alive for nearly thirty years, been doing hard work over a decade, still looked like a kid. I just knew I had to leave, that there was some bedevilment with me, that either folks would get suspicious or I would infect them...something bad.

Those thoughts like he was talking to himself—

Talking to himself in an Irish accent.

Anne would continue to send reports of progress and her opinion that Price should be put back on duty to the Captain. The cop thanked her but felt uneasy: He knew he was over 400 years old, knew their kind was called *Aeterni*, but beyond that his memories were still mostly a void.

"Be patient," Anne said. "We've seen this before; you'll hear a song or see a place in a movie or smell a certain food and more memories will return. They're locked away, not gone."

"But, you could tell me my past." He said.

"It can't work that way, it would be too much too quickly," she smiled. "Your memories have to come back on their own, organically."

"Organically," Charlie repeated.

He walked to the door of her office and then turned back towards the therapist.

"Is this why I am hypersensitive, why things that don't bother other people overwhelm me?"

"Probably, you do seem hypersensitive, though; see it as a tool---it may save your life someday...it probably already has."

Charlie nodded and walked out, overwhelmed, trying to process everything---

It may save your life someday.

Price had been a soldier in Afghanistan in the 1800s; with information Anne had shared he could identify that as a memory and not a weird dream. Britain had been fighting over there, he had probably joined the British Army or something.

Afghanistan—why did he have such a strong connection? First his time there in the 1800s and then in the US Army in 2002—maybe it meant *something*, maybe it was a coincidence.

Back home, he sat at the piano and closed his eyes as if doing so would bring back more memories.

Your memories have to come back on their own, organically.

Hopefully it would happen soon.

The Sentra

Price couldn't sleep. He put on the previous day's clothes and strapped on the Ruger. It was time for a walk. As always there was no destination; Charlie just ended up where he ended up. This time it was to the street where he had torn his favorite slacks. Price looked down and realized he was wearing the same pants. The sense of deja vu that overcame him made it feel as an army of insects were moving over his skin---

Something was wrong, something in the world was off.

A car motor, a tremendous bass signature growing louder. The sound of the engine was ragged and the bass made the car rattle. It was a Nissan Sentra from the early 90s that had been lowered and primered. The fact he had never seen the car before increased Charlie's anxiety. The Sentra pulled up alongside him, the passenger window came down. They were kids---was the driver even old enough to drive? She was wearing shades and a fedora pulled low as if to disguise her age. Focusing on the driver was a mistake, maybe the last mistake Price would make. The boy in the passenger seat had pulled a .38 revolver from the area behind the gearshift. While Price had been focusing on the driver the boy had crossed the arm over his chest and aimed the gun at the cop. At the end of the arm was the hateful face of Charlie Russell, the other arm was still in a sling.

Then: Charlie Russell being put on a gurney by paramedics as he whimpered and grimaced about his broken arm.

Now: Price understood that he had three seconds to live...

PART TWO: THE HERMIT

The Ravens

The ravens led him to the dead man---they were circling as if they had spotted a tortoise or a dead jackrabbit. Tracking their orbit the hermit climbed a rise and saw something that didn't fit in with the basalt and scrub; a form the size of a thimble that became the size of a plastic army man. A minute later the army man was large enough that he could tell that it was walking.
It was a person, a dead man or woman.
The only people you saw around there were usually lost. It wasn't the sort of lost like you get in a strange city where ducking into a shop for directions is an option; being lost in the desert often ends in bleached bones that may or may not be found. You take a wrong turn, you get your car stuck, and soon you end up in a situation that you cannot fix and God will not pluck you from no matter how much you beg. A panic sets in that clouds your ability to see your options and the clock runs down. The hermit just stood there watching the stranger for a couple of minutes. A good guy would have waved and called out to let the dead man know he wasn't a dead man after all. A good guy would have gone over with a canteen and reassurances as refreshing as cool water. He had never believed that he was a good guy.
Watching the tiny figure moving in the distance the observer felt everything dark a man can feel: Resentment in every color for the intrusion, the hubris, and lack of respect for a wild, beautiful place. The hermit contemplated letting nature take its course; turning around and walking home as if he had seen nothing.
In the end he did just that.

Live or Die

As he walked back home his most recent dreams came back into focus: An abandoned office park. People with guns chasing him. He had a pistol on him but understood he couldn't use it on his pursuers. Why? It probably had to do with a memory linked to the dream. The problem was that memory was somewhere out of reach, floating in the darkness.

Maybe the stranger was meant to die. The hermit wasn't religious, not in a Christian/going to church manner, but he believed in fate and karma. Maybe it was his or her time; it was a brutal thing to think and he felt guilty for having such cold thoughts...cold like the water he should be filling a jug with. *Should be*—what had the stranger expected? You go out into the deep desert, act stupid, and you expect to be rescued? Why? So you can go off and do more stupid things? Maybe your stupidity ruins other lives. The hermit had those thoughts and didn't fight the anger attached to them until he tasted the poison. He struggled to see the stranger as another human being and allowed his conscience to run a slideshow: Scattered bones. Sobbing loved ones. Said loved ones frantically calling the authorities over and over for news they'd never get---unless the hermit filled the jug with water and drove out to where he had seen the dead man or woman. He saw those things in his mind but still felt nothing. The hermit may as well been an animatron as he filled the jug and walked out to his truck.

The hermit set the jug on the passenger floor and stared at it. That water was the dead man's life; he could either keep it from him or take it to him. The power felt in that moment was unsettling, heavy like a gun in one's hand. In the dream he had been *pursued*, but that wasn't the way it really was, was it? He started the truck and began driving towards where he had seen the ravens.

The Wash

The stranger was in a sandy wash so the final distance between
them had to be closed on foot.

Words...they were wild, not wanting to be caught---

The man with the water jug worked on putting together words to
say to the dead person. He paused, scratched at his beard, gripped
the handle of the jug like a hand he was contemplating breaking.
It wasn't too late to turn back. The hermit closed his eyes:
Sobbing loved ones. Innocents who hadn't been completely
fucking stupid by sauntering off into the desert. He still felt
nothing but managed to get walking again. Closing the distance
revealed a man near sixty with sweaty but neatly combed hair.
The way he was smiling it was as if they were meeting on a leafy
residential street and not a place that can kill you. The sight of
him was jarring---usually it's men in their twenties full of
testosterone who challenge the elements, not guys who appear to
be retirement age.

"Boy, am I glad to see *you*!" The stranger was chuckling, his voice
strong.

The trespasser was sunburned and had sweat stains on his shirt
but otherwise looked fine. The rescuer's hand kneaded the handle
of the water bottle, his eyes hard dots watching the stranger's
body for any sudden movements or changes in posture. Handing
the water over meant being close enough for the stranger to grab a
wrist and pull out a knife from his waistband. Offering the bottle,
his hand as far away from his body as possible; the stranger shook
his head and said something unintelligible---it could have been a
thank you, it could have been a confession. There was a smell to
the stranger: Not just sweat, a familiar cologne. The hermit
couldn't identify the perfume but he knew it and his intuition

was that the scent was a bad omen. The two men stood in silence as the older man ignored the bottle and took in the surrounding escarpments. Why was he looking at them? Hadn't they been mocking him for a couple of days or however long he had been stuck out there?

"Your car break down or something?" The hermit asked.

The man looked at the hermit for a few moments; something in his eyes reminded his rescuer of the circling ravens.

"Got stuck."

An obvious lie---they were standing in a place where people easily vanish with only lies in-between them. The lie made bringing the words out even more of a struggle.

"That tends to happen out here. I'm guessing you don't have a phone signal."

The trespasser shook his head. He was determined to make eye contact with his rescuer who wanted anything but that. Was the stranger dangerous? Would he pull out some hidden weapon, use it, and steal the truck? There was a rifle behind the front seat; it was a life's journey from where the two men stood.

"Do you think you need a doctor?" The hermit asked.

Not caring, reciting lines from tv shows and movies out of obligation.

"No. I would like to get out of here, though."

"I can take you to Beatty."

The two of them walked towards the truck. The hermit tried to keep the stranger off his back, glancing around at the escarpments to remain aware of the location of the stranger's hands, changes in posture.

There is a survival knife under the seat.

It was good news but good news with dark bunting---could he stab someone? Stabbing someone wasn't like shooting them; there was the resistance of multiple layers of fabric and flesh...and being so close you can't escape the reality of what you're doing to another human being. The hermit imagined himself faltering with the blade and the trespasser chuckling as he gutted his rescuer like a fish.

What were you really doing out here? Are they going to find a skeleton in that wash someday? Were you burying some treasure that you killed for?

The rescuer's pulse played a kettle drum. Desperate to bring the tempo down he imagined who or what had made the tracks that meandered through the wash.

There was a vision of nineteenth century pioneers: Lost. Dehydrated. Fucked.

The stranger was leading them wearing a chin beard and that dangerous smile.

The hermit felt as if he were skipping hand in hand with a madness that had entwined fingers like vines around his.

"Son, I owe you a debt of gratitude."

He opened the passenger door to climb in; it felt like a violation.

"Don't mention it."

Locked jaw words earning a happy chuckle. The town seemed a million miles away.

Twilight

The hermit was sitting in his pickup with the jug of water on the passenger floor. Had he rescued the dead man? Had that really happened or had he been daydreaming what would occur if he went out to find the stranger? There was the faint scent of cologne in the truck; satisfied, the hermit took the keys out of the ignition and walked inside.

Settling in for the hottest hours of the day he tried to remember the last time he had a conversation with another human being. It had to have been at the store in Beatty--a week before? Two weeks? Two weeks was normally as long as he could go without exchanging a few words, sharing space---even casually---with another person. He would have never suspected ever needing human contact before living in isolation. Out there everything usually made sense, felt *right---*
A flashback of the older man's face and the breezy smile that didn't belong on it. Had his face looked like that? He was imagining the stranger clean shaven when he could have sworn there was some gray stubble. Outsiders had been rare out there when he had bought the land. Now they were setting their alien feet on his sand and raising their flags was becoming a common occurrence. The regular world just wouldn't leave the hermit to his slow, beautifully designed death.

When twilight came the hermit poured a mason jar full of chilled water and walked outside. The condensation was cool on his hand as he stood in a respectful silence as the afternoon died. Not one sunrise or sunset has been missed since the shack had been finished. The light was one of the reasons for moving out there--the light and the solitude. When the darkness was full and complete the hermit climbed on the roof to stare at the stars. He could not name them, had no idea where any constellations are aside from the Big Dipper--his enjoyment was blissfully ignorant. The desert is a place you go to see light in a way you could have never imagined it---

The desert is a place you go to die: It is a beautiful world where death is a shrug and you realize how small you really are.

It was a cathedral, it was a casual killing field, it was his home.

Prints

There was a truck on the ridge when he carried his first cup of coffee outside. Maybe they were security people on patrol or maybe they were scouting for places to mine. Seeing the sun glint off the white pickup, the Hermit remembered that he had dreamt of the office park again; being pursued down breezeways. There had been bag lunch left on a bench. Stopping to see what was inside he had heard running footsteps closing on where he stood.

Aside from the trucks on the ridge there had been peace since he had kept the Promise. Memories would return, bad ones, but they had become frail and easily sent away--the *then*.
Now: An older man who should have looked scared and beaten down smiling as if on a stroll down a tree-lined street.
Then...No. He had drained the blood of those memories--literally--they had no right to life. Shadows were collecting and the fading light was beginning to give their shapes definition. He would find the light switch and cast them out, he had to. The hermit thought of the stranger in the wash again. Had he been wearing a light blue shirt? Why did he want to say he had been wearing a tie? That made no sense, maybe his mind was going. Getting altizimers or Parkinsons was a fear of his---losing his ability to take care of himself in a place that would show no mercy.

The next morning the hermit drove his truck out to where he had come across the smiling man. After putting two camelbaks over his shoulders he set out; something was unsettled and he had to determine what had stirred things loose. It was a few minutes before seven and sweat beads were forming on his skin, he had maybe four hours round trip before the heat became unpleasant. *Then*: Night. A small car full of teenagers trying to look hard. Him focusing on the wrong thing...

Now: Stopping in his tracks and willing the memory away.

He didn't want to find prints; finding prints made the Smiling Man real. Was he? Or, had he been alone for too long with a guilt that was always denied. Were those footprints next to a Mormon Tea bush? He thought he saw them: Big shoes. Clumsy way of walking. No, it was just a place where a small animal had laid down. A circling raven called, probably the same one that liked to sit on his roof. It was half of a bonded pair, the hermit liked to feed them even if they shit on his truck and shack if he forgot to share his stale bread. Where had the man been walking from? If he went in the general direction then he'd have to eventually find tracks.

After a few minutes the hermit came to the entrance of a box canyon. There hadn't been any tracks or signs of a stranded vehicle. A decent gravel road led nearly to the mouth of the box canyon. It would have been impossible to get stuck on that road--what if the Smiling Man had gone off into open country? What if the mining company had come out and towed his vehicle away? There was less than three hours before the sun became merciless. It wasn't a raven circling, the wings hadn't moved; it was a drone imitating the flight of a bird. He started walking back the way he had come.

Then: A boy screaming as he slapped at his ruined eye socket. No, he hadn't screamed, just convulsed---he was already dying.

Now: The drone imitating a bird flew off to the north. Now he was sure he could hear the motor. Why hadn't he heard it before?

Then: Children screaming in the small space of a car as one of them died--the smell of burnt flesh and blood...

Now: The hermit stopped, closed his eyes, and willed the memory away.

Battery

A snippet of Toto's "Hold the Line"--a text was coming in. The source was a number, not a name. The Government was testing its emergency system again. The hermit suspected they were testing connections, making sure they could always track him and listen when he was talking to himself. The text reminded him of electricity which reminded him about the batteries charged by the solar panels--how long had it been since he had added water? Yes, he was overdue. Eleven days--since adding water, not since the last email.

Then: Moving up another narrow canyon, with men that time, coming upon the saddest shape he would ever see. How could something so beautiful end like that?

Now: He cursed himself for following the circling ravens the day before.

Then: A snub nose .38 coming up. It would be months before he would recognize how weathered it was, how it was more dangerous to the person pointing it than him. A shot. No, an explosion. Hard faces changing into the children they really were--even the girl behind the wheel was only fifteen. The boy he had saved couldn't have been saved after all. The hermit had watched him die. The coming months there would be no doubt, no *what really happened* moments: The boy was dead.

Now: The hermit pulled up a panel in the floor and checked the batteries. The water level was fine. He reached further into the darkness risking whatever cooled itself in the shade to exert self-preservation. Another box was squeezed around the deep cycle batteries and into the light. He had not looked in the box since--months? Years? His old life was in there, the few things he risked bringing into his new life after fulfilling the Promise.

The Smiling Man

Boy, am I glad to see you!
The details of the Smiling Man kept changing: Blue shirt. Pale green shirt. Tie, no tie. Southwest accent. Slight Southern accent, maybe Alabama with some time in Missouri. The only consistency was that the face was familiar. Had he imagined the lost stranger? The only footprints out there were his. He wanted to say no, almost desperately--imagining encounters was a sign that maybe the isolation was affecting his mind.

Another twilight, another time of the heat dissipating to make way for the chill that drifted across the desert at night. He took stale bread outside and scattered it. A raven was nearby but didn't come for it. It was watching him. To the hermit it seemed as if the bird were *reading* him.
"Why did you lead me to him?"
The raven continued to stare without saying anything.

Clues

The Smiling Man wasn't an illusion. No, you can't smell illusions just as you cannot smell ghosts. The hermit knew all the smells in his truck; that body spray or cologne was not one of them. The scent was proof that he was not losing his mind but still needed more proof. The mining company may have towed the stranger's vehicle. The hermit didn't want to deal with the mining company. He was concerned they would ask him not to trespass on their property during his walks. Until they did, he could plead ignorance if confronted during his wanderings. What would have been the Smiling Man's options? The nearest bus depot was in Las Vegas. Logically, there weren't any taxis to take him the hundred-seventeen and a half miles but he might have bribed someone. Whatever answers there were awaited him in town.

The cafe might have been the best place to inquire about a stranger looking for rides but the cafe was overflowing with faces and voices and smells. The hermit had heard that people sometimes hitched out of the filling station. It was a haphazard place full of random snacks and magazines and ghosts of a time when the shop did repairs; the scents of drying grease and oil. The owner was an acerbic fat man with a tendency to play rock music from the 1970s in the garage. That morning, instead of Thin Lizzy or Bachman Turner Overdrive slow hip hop was playing. The rapper was familiar but the hermit couldn't place him. Instead of the owner a boyman in his early twenties with an amatuer beard was behind the counter. Toby---his name was Toby, right? The boyman was staring at his phone and moving his thumbs as explosions and screams in miniature added accents to the music coming from the next room. He was not aware of the man walking into the store until that man was standing next to the counter staring at him. Toby(?) looked up with a lazy but genuine looking smile.

"What's up, Boss? We don't usually get you in town twice in one week."

"I brought someone in a couple of days ago, wanted to make sure he had gotten to Vegas alright."

It was surprising how easily the words were coming; maybe he really was becoming a new person. There was nothing to worry about--he had not imagined the stranger and there he was having a regular conversation.

"Stranger needed a ride? No...you check the cafe?"

The Cafe: Did he really have to go into the cafe to verify that the Smiling Man had been real?

"No. That's a good idea, though, thanks."

Toby smiled and nodded and was back in his game.

Boomvest, that was what it was; everyone under 30 seemed to be playing it. Another track by the same rapper started up. Gilbert had to know who it was.

"Hey, who is this you're listening to?"

"Low2Dipz---you like it?"

"No."

The hermit walked down the street towards the cafe. He had been honest about his reaction to the music and honesty was a good path to follow but--his tone, the way he had spit out *no*--had he been harsh? Toby was a good kid, didn't deserve someone being a dick.

Relax. He was so into his game that he probably didn't even hear you.

Yes, that was probably true. Now he could move on.

The cafe was seventy percent full. He could hear laughter and voices through the glass and it made him stop and clench and unclench his right hand trying to dissipate the building tension. *You have to go in. Inside there is confirmation about the Smiling Man coming to town and asking about a ride.*

But what if no one remembered the Smiling Man? Nothing about the fellow really stood out except maybe to people like Gilbert. Did he really need someone in the crowded restaurant to confirm his existence? No, the evidence was right there in his truck--smells don't lie.

Hunters

Then: Smells don't lie. There was a strange smell in the truck, a cologne or soap he didn't use. Therefore, he *had* the Smiling Man in his truck and wasn't imagining things.
Now: Unsure, chiding himself for not just finding the will and the words to go into the cafe and inquire about the stranger.

He sat on the edge of the bed and hit a couple of notes on the piano. The sound was soothing, crushed the sparks. Peace came and he climbed into bed and read until he could feel dreams drifting towards him in the darkness.

He was back in the office park. No, it was an apartment complex. An abandoned one with broken glass, weeds coming up through the walkway, and graffiti. Someone had sprayed *Low2Dipz Ryder* below and an angry looking face. Old R & B was coming from somewhere--he couldn't decide whether it was the Spinners or the Temptations. His pursuers---
No, he wasn't being pursued, he was hunting someone and the Ruger was in his hand.

Ravens arguing outside woke him from the dream. The hermit thought of the morning when they had led him to the Smiling Man. The details of the dream were fading. No, the dream would return full strength another night as it had been coming in stages the past few years. The dreams had taken shape back when he lived in a city and had followed him out into the wilderness.

The sun wasn't fully over the mountains to the east when he took his coffee on the porch. One more beautiful morning; at some

124

point he would run out of them. How many were left? Hundreds? A couple thousand?

No, he was being too modest, unwilling to face the truth. There was another truck on the ridge. Had they seen a tiny version of the Smiling Man down in the wash? He finished his coffee and went inside.

Buyers

Toto's "Hold the Line" alerted him to a text from an unknown
source. He picked up his phone dreading another veiled threat
from the government. The message was worse--it was a realtor.
The one who worked with the mining company.

*Mr. Franks, I need to speak with you about your property. I am
working with a business entity that has asked me to put forward a
very generous offer. I apologize for the text but I don't have a phone
number for you. If I do not receive a text back can I visit in person
in two days?*

Two days? The text had been delayed...two days. At any time
there would be the sound of a car or truck coming up the road.
Locals understood that you didn't just drive up a private road and
not expect a load of buckshot over your roof. Realtors tended to
be more brazen. Franks texted back with the desperation of
someone falling asleep willing away a nightmare:

"Thank you for reaching out. Not interested."

Would that be enough or would they ignore the text and just
show up? He poured the coffee from his thermos into his cup.
Toto played again, the guitar break this time; it was an amazing
guitar break, Franks had always loved the different textures.

"Hi, Mr. Franks! I appreciate your response. My client would
really like for you to at least consider their offer. You are the last
piece of the puzzle."

He already knew that. His acres had been bought before the
B.L.M. had privately sold their holdings in the area. The mining
company had bought up every acre of B.L.M. land and all the
other parcels---aside from Gilbert's.

Then: A mosque near the river of the city he had lived in. They
had developed on three sides of it down by the river. The Imam

,

had refused to sell, had held on strong even as construction went on around his mosque day to week to year.

Now: How long until the inquiries became less polite? How long until the mining company used its resources to get the hermit kicked off his land? More importantly, where would he go?

"Sorry. No. That is my final word. Forever."

They wouldn't like that. He imagined the realtor scowling as he or she looked into their phone in response to what *that weird hermit* had written. How would they intimidate him? His shack was legal. Maybe they would cite him for having a composting toilet instead of a septic tank. Maybe they would shine spotlights in the dead of night or play loud music. Maybe they would dump their garbage on his land in the dead of night.

Those were concerns for another day.

The Ridge

It had been three days since Franks had first seen a truck on the ridge. There had been ravens making noise that day, too; they were probably upset because that was *their* ridge. The same birds had scolded Gilbert when he had begun building his shack. At first it was just trucks to the north but soon there were the drones imitating birds and now there were sounds coming from the south, construction sounds. He had left the city to escape all the noise and roaring machines but the world had changed and there was no getting away from them. He had not allowed himself to accept that. Even if accepting it would have brought him peace, accepting it seemed impossible.

The hermit shut himself in for the hottest hours of the day. The internet was down and he had no interest in reading. Being surrounded by strangers with their noises and eyes made him anxious. The anxiety was potent enough to make him wonder if it would build until it took over his life; one more crazy man in a wild and unforgiving place. He thought of the mosque in the city to distract himself. When they had built it the mosque had been a couple of miles from the city. It had been a beautiful place, a tranquil setting for communing with God. Decades passed and the city built up all around the mosque. The Imam held on until right before Franks had left the city. They had been determined to provide a beautiful place for area Muslims to gather despite the noise but the city had changed in other ways. The rest of the country saw it as a Liberal city, an open-minded place, and maybe it was...in most ways. The Muslims had been feeling less and less welcome. Streets they knew and places they had taken comfort in were no longer havens from all the suspicion and prejudice. The

Imam gave up and took his people to another location. The mosque was torn down and the developers built a beige block of cement and glass where it had stood. The hermit had trespassed to steal decorative tile from the ruins; it served as the base for his wood burning stove.

The hermit walked out to his truck. He sat behind the wheel and closed the door despite the brutal heat; it was as hot as those Bible people said Hell was. Hell is not a location, though, Hell is feelings and memories and anxieties. Gilbert understood that; he understood it and accepted it just as he finally accepted that the only smells in the truck were his.

I could stay in here. It would get bad but eventually I will pass out and die.

It seemed a shame to have such a thought in such a beautiful place but he couldn't help it. He thought back a few days, to the place the circling ravens had led him. The Smiling Man was out there growing larger and more detailed as Franks approached. An older man with beads of sweat on his forehead from being out in the heat. No, the beads of sweat were from the anxiety that fear was bringing on.

The man was anxious because he knew *why* Franks was standing before him

Then: Two short films, one of discovering the body of what had been a beautiful young woman raped and murdered in the desert. And then, mercifully, Celeste sitting on her bed smiling. He could smell her shampoo in his dreams.

Now: Ravens were circling in the distance; something was on the other side of the ridge. They had found something worth their time, maybe a tortoise or a dead jackrabbit. Franks felt sweat covering his body as he breathed in heat.

Then: The Smiling Man wasn't in a blue short sleeve button down shirt or a green one, he was in a dark blue suit. An expensive one. He was not standing in a remote wash but in a parking garage next to an SUV that had cost more than the hermit's house. The original thought had been to gut shoot the man in the suit and take him somewhere to suffer out the last days of his life just as Celeste had suffered.

Now: It was hard to focus on the present time, the heat was causing him to drift. Franks set a hand on the hot dashboard and pain was enough to cut through his disorientation.

Then: The man in the suit was standing in front of him after years of research and making himself talk to strangers and false leads. Here he was, the man who had started the chain of events that led to a beautiful girl dead in a remote desert canyon. He had no idea why a gun was being leveled at him. The man in the suit thought it was just another robbery and was babbling that Franks could take what he wanted and they could even go to an ATM and-- Then there was a pop, and a second---one shot in the left eye and another where the heart should be and the talking stopped and the man sank to the ground. That was it, it was all over but wiping the little automatic down and dropping it near the body. There was no remorse or triumph or guilt, not even the relief he had hoped for--there was no sensation whatsoever. Franks had taken the dead man's wallet and watch and walked away.

Now: The ravens called again. The hermit closed his eyes and put his hands on the steering wheel. Everything was getting calm, even the heat was bothering him less. Franks imagined that, if he could hold on a little bit longer, Celeste would open the passenger door, climb in, and sit beside him.

PART III: THE HEATWAVE

The Bar

The man looked up at the shelves behind the bar: Glenlivet. Jameson. Dewers. They all looked good, even the Ten High on a lower shelf. He must have been making a face because the bartender walked over with a frown of his own.

"You okay?"

"Yeah..."

"Cause you look like something is bothering you."

The man toyed with his glass of tonic water, lifting it as if to take a drink and then setting it down.

"I had some weird dreams when I was in the hospital," the customer started carefully, unsure if he wanted to share what was troubling him.

The bartender just stared at him for a few seconds before leaning forward and speaking.

"You can't just leave it there man..."

"The thing is, it wasn't like dreams, it felt real; it *feels* real."

He took a drink of his tonic water. The bartender was summoned to the end of the bar where he got a Budweiser for another customer. Someone in a booth complained about the heat in the bar.

"Sorry, boss," the bartender called across the room. "None of us were prepared for it being 115 degrees. I got the swamp cooler on, it's the best I can do."

"It smells like mold in here," the customer continued, a sour look on his face. "Hot mold, cooking mold..."

"That's all I can do," the bartender replied with a pursed smile and a shrug.

He walked back to the man sipping tonic water. It was clear from his face that he couldn't decide which was worse, the customer talking about the hot mold smell or the weird conversation with his friend.

"You remember that deal with the kids?" The man with the tonic water asked.

"Yeah, you saved them," the bartender smiled warmly.

"Well...something about the stress of that situation, I started having daydreams—daydreams that were making me believe my memories were false."

"I don't get it," the bartender frowned.

The customer looked around to make sure no one was listening. "I started having daydreams about a long time ago, like almost 200 years ago. But they were memories or felt like memories and it was driving me nuts."

"Wait: These were the dreams you had in the hospital, right?"

"I guess," the customer said, unsure if the description *dreams* was accurate, "Like I said, they felt like memories, not dreams. This went on for a week and then I had to visit a psychiatrist because of the situation with the kids."

"I remember that," the bartender smiled. "You told me about it."

"Did I tell you that she told me that I had a rare genetic condition? That I had been born four hundred years ago...yeah, you're looking at me funny, I know how nuts this sounds."

"It's a crazy dream, dude."

"It gets weirder. I became this hermit living in the desert who had killed a bunch of people to get revenge for killing someone I loved—"

"Wait, now that makes sense. I mean, what happened to your sister in Afghanistan."

"Yeah, she's my sister," the customer said softly. "*Was*."

"Dude," the bartender said gently. "You were shot in the head, you were in a coma for three weeks...I think some weird dreams are to be expected."

The customer took a sip of his tonic water, looked up at the Glenlivet again—he really wanted a drink, a *real* drink.

"Usually, you can have a dream and it's clear it was a dream," the man with the tonic water said. "This feels different, like I was experiencing *memories* and not dreams."

The bartender was unsure how to reply. He began wiping the surface of the bar with a towel as if rubbing it would summon a genie with all the answers.

Like how to talk to friends dealing with weird shit.

"Charlie...a bullet hit your brain...I don't know what to tell you, man; I imagine you'll be thinking and dreaming of weird shit the rest of your life."

"Maybe."

Charlie forced himself to look away from the shelf of whiskey bottles.

"I just needed to talk about it," he continued. "Get it out of my system before I talk to the psychiatrist."

"Psychiatrist?"

"Yeah, they need to evaluate me before I can go back to active duty."

"That's part of the deal?"

"Yeah, anytime you experience a trauma—"

"Like being shot in the head?" The bartender winked.

"Like being shot in the head," Charlie smiled back.

A customer had walked up with an empty tumbler, the bartender switched his focus. Charlie frowned; it *did* smell like hot mold in there.

Dawn

A text from Dawn Mendez; all texts from her were dangerous. She asked how his recovery was going, if he would be able to return to work soon. A friendly text; she was his partner and she was his friend. Charlie kept telling himself he could see her that way, that he could push away the memories of how her hair had gotten in her face as she hovered over him, in his bed. Her face had been sweaty as she looked down at him fondly then with an expression full of pleasure.

This can never happen again.

And he had nodded, agreeing; it *could* never happen again, Dawn was married, married and pregnant. She had been self conscious about that, her belly swelled by the child inside, but he had assured her that was beautiful and the way she smiled Price could tell she had appreciated that.

This can never happen again.

But it had; he'd be home, looking out the window for crows or messing around on the piano and he'd hear the kettle drum, Mendez knocking on the security door. It had happened three times and each time his partner had reiterated it could never happen again and Charlie had agreed—

And then she stopped coming. And then the baby had been born. Days and then weeks passed. He kept hoping he'd hear the kettle drum and felt self loathing for that: Dawn was a married woman. He never should have messed around with her in the first place...certainly shouldn't have developed feelings for her that he didn't dare name.

You have no right to feel those things just as you had no right to be involved with her; suffering through those feelings is a just punishment.

And now she was texting to check on him, as a friend. And he responded...as a friend. Eventually he would get past all the other stupid stuff in his head...those feelings for her. He wrote back that he had an appointment with the psychiatrist, that he expected to be back on duty within a few days. After sending the message he just stood there, holding his phone and staring at the screen, waiting for her response.

You are such an idiot. It's been months; the two of you had fun and she's moved on...you need to, as well.

But that logic didn't stop him from just holding his phone, waiting for her reply...or maybe she'd just show up and knock on the door....

Idiot...you are a fucking idiot.

She did write back, no words, just a smiley face emoji.

Was she glad he'd be back because he was a good partner or because of something else?

Idiot...just stop...stop being such a fucking idiot. It's too hot for this crap.

The Precinct

Charlie had never been invisible at work as much as he would
have liked to have been: The cop had always been the "guy who
was too quiet" and now he was "the guy who had been shot in
the head." At least it was cool or at least comfortable in the police
station, the City had priority to run the air conditioners full blast.
As Charlie walked in the precinct, a young man was being
brought in. The kid wasn't in cuffs but you could tell by the
closeness of the officer who was bringing him in that the young
man was under arrest—at least that was Charlie's impression. The
young man looked over at Price with a nod.
"We're just running the clock down, bro," he said.
He was looking intently at Charlie---was he expecting a response?
"What?" Charlie replied.
The young man was no longer looking at Price's face, he was
looking up, possibly at where the bullet had struck Price's skull.
"You know what I said," the young man smirked, he had acne
scars and his cheeks and his dark brown hair looked oily.
"It's too hot for your hully gully," the cop next to him said,
grabbing the young man's arm and leading him through a door.
Price did not follow them.

Price got lost. The building was old, one of the oldest buildings in
the City, a maze of illogical corridors and rooms that could only
be accessed through other rooms. He walked down an empty
corridor, then one teeming with cops, and then another empty
corridor. Dawn was in one of the crowded ones, stopping to
drink from one of the ancient drinking fountains. She appeared
to sense him and looked over with a smile.
"You here for your appointment?"

"Yeah," he made a point to keep a friend distance, keep the feelings she brought up buried or at least buried enough that she couldn't pick up on them. "I have no idea where the therapists have their offices."

"The basement, I think," she frowned. "At least it will be cooler down there."

"Good point," he nodded. "How have you been?"

She looked taken aback by that: *Does she see that as a personal question? Does she think I am asking as the guy she had sex with?* And then Mendez appeared relaxed and friendly again.

"Okay. They partnered me with Marsten while you were out; you know how people who are racist try to overcompensate, insisting they aren't racist which just makes it more clear they are racist?"

"Oh, yeah," Charlie laughed a little. He could smell her shampoo, was pretty sure it was Suave. She seemed to be enjoying the conversation maybe—

Stop. Just...stop.

"I'd better find my psychiatrist," he said.

She looked disappointed by that but quickly covered it up.

"Yeah, and I'd better find my racist partner....*temporary* partner."

"See you around."

Charlie forced himself to walk off, it was the only thing he could do.

Evaluation

The shrink was like any other shrink Price had visited:
Nondescript clothes. Gentle expression and calm demeanor.
Softly spoken yet probing inquiries. Charlie turned a machine on
in his head to answer the psychiatrist's questions how he thought
they were supposed to be answered—he kept seeing the kids in
the car, the kid who shot him. All the details were there, down to
the driver's nipples visible through her light blue sweatshirt and
the gun blowing up in Charlie Russell's face.
Charlie, a bullet hit your brain...I don't know what to tell you...
True, that had to be it....right? But—
The injury could fuck with his memories but could it mess with
his *instincts*? His instincts told him that his memories were not to
be trusted.
The dialogue went on and on in a loop as he smiled pleasantly
and made up answers for the psychiatrist. She kept mopping the
sweat off her brow with a cotton cloth but said nothing about the
heat.

Driving home, the air conditioner in the old Mercedes struggled
to keep up with the heat and the cop had to turn it down when
the temp gauge pushed up towards "H." The woodgrain
appliqué on the dash had begun peeling due to the glue holding it
on melting; the smell of forty year old paste made the cop feel
even more discombobulated. Pedestrian traffic was scant as few
people in the town were accustomed to the heat they were
experiencing. It was eighty-seven in the house when the cop got
home; all he had was a wall air conditioner in the living
room---he'd probably sleep on the couch that night. After getting
a glass of ice water, Charlie's thoughts went back to his session

with the psychiatrist—she would have to report to HR who would report to the Captain or at least that was what Price had heard. The cop sat at the piano and plinked out a few notes but he was too distracted to really play—

Something was in the backyard. He grabbed the .357 and held it at his right hip as he moved aside the blinds to look through the kitchen window. An orange cat was sitting next to a rock and looking up at the window with a neutral cat sort of expression---it was as if the animal had been expecting Charlie to look through the blinds. He had never seen a cat in his yard before—

Is that true? Or, did the injury erase my memory? For all I know that's my cat and it's wondering why the fuck I haven't let it in.

No, there was no smell of cat shit in the house, no food or bowls or toys or anything you associate with a pet or even a neighborhood creature you left food out for. But, that cat was sure staring at the window, like it was expecting Charlie to feed it or at least pay attention to it. The cop tucked the gun in the back of his waistband and went to the back door. When he opened it, the cat ran off.

Special Case

A text came in overnight that Price was reinstated and instructed him to attend the morning briefing. Getting dressed that morning, Charlie noticed that his pants had been mended which confused him: When and why had he sewn on them? They were his favorite slacks, it seemed odd that he would have forgotten tearing them. Distracted, he didn't have an appetite and struggled to remember how he had rent his trousers while drinking his coffee.

The morning briefing: Uniforms talked amongst themselves as did plainclothes, mostly about the heat and how it was predicted to be 117 that day—had it ever been that hot in the city before? Charlie stood alone. All their smells and the waves of their murmurs didn't bother him as much as they had in the past.
I guess getting shot in the head wasn't an entirely bad thing.
He made the effort to look attentive and engaged as the sergeant briefed the shift and gave out assignments.
"And Price," the Sergeant nodded at Charlie. "The Captain is assigning a special case to you; you'll get an email shortly."
Some of the plainclothes and uniforms looked over at Price; they had been doing so since the beginning of the briefing.
The guy who was shot in the head. Price, again, was surprised that all the attention wasn't playing on his anxiety. *Most guys shot in the head you don't see standing around and looking attentive,* he mused, *maybe that's it.*
After being dismissed, Charlie walked to his cubicle, remembering how Dawn looked at the drinking fountain, hoping he'd run into her.

*Just...stop. It's been over two months. You need to get over it, be
cool—*
And maybe if you play it cool she'll knock on your door again...
Hopeless, I am absolutely fucking hopeless.

He logged into his official computer and found the email the
sergeant had sent. It was for a missing persons case—why was it
being given to him? He had never handled a missing person's case
before. Then he noticed the Afghani names of the people who
had reported the missing person.
Maybe they only speak Pashto.
Charlie needed more coffee but worried about another cup on an
empty stomach; what was he going to have for lunch, anyway?
He read more of the case: The missing person was a fifteen year
old female, the desk officer had noted that her family was
Arab-American. No, the last name definitely sounded Afghani.
Price looked down at his mobile, even if his anxiety was lower
than usual he still hated talking on the telephone. Did he start
with English or Pasto? How long had it been since he spoke the
latter? Would he be rusty?
You're stalling, just make the call.
"Yes?" A man's voice, heavily accented.
"Yes, sir," Price began. "I'm Inspector Price from the police, you
reported your daughter missing."
A long pause, maybe *hello* was the extent of the man's English.
Price repeated what he had said in Pashto. The man was holding
the phone out and arguing with someone else, a woman by the
sound of it. Their conversation sounded like Pashto but maybe it
was Dari...it had been years since Afghanistan.
"Inspector Price, you are calling about my daughter," a woman's
voice, her English less accented.

"Yes, I would like to arrange a time to come and speak to you both."

She held the phone out and argued with the man in what had to be Dari.

"Can you come by at six this evening?" The woman asked.

"Yes."

She Was a Good Girl

The family lived in a subdivision from the early 70s's, a Toyota Camry and a Ford Econoline parked in the driveway. The van stumped Price—did the father have some kind of business that required a cargo van? There had to be an explanation but it nagged at him.

"Very old car for police," the husband grunted at the front door, looking over the cop's shoulder. He was somewhere in his forties with a spreading bald spot and a mustache. His hair was a rich brown that appeared to have come from a bottle.

"It's my personal car," Price explained.

The man just looked at him; Charlie felt frustrated because, although he knew a little Dari, it was not enough to hold a conversation.

"Please, we are letting heat into the house," the man stepped back and gestured for the cop to walk in.

The house smelled stale, closed in; it looked clean just not aired out enough. A woman, presumably the mother of the missing girl, walked into the living room and nodded at Price. Like her husband the woman was around 40 with a veil over her long black hair. She wore a paisley patterned dress that came down to her calves and brown, leather sandals. Price could tell that the parents hadn't slept in a couple of days. He wanted to feel empathy for them---

The daughter is their Celeste.

"I am Inspector Price," he said, looking at both off them in turn. "I apologize, I barely speak Dari. Will English work or would you like me to schedule a translator?"

"We are American citizens." The wife looked annoyed. "You think we do not speak English?"

"I apologize." Those words were so firm and inflexible they barely made it out of his mouth.

"Our language *is* Dari, but I can speak English with you," she looked contrite, probably for snapping at Price.

"Okay...well, tell me about your daughter."

Her anger returned; Charlie could see she was so frustrated *her* words wouldn't come.

"I'm sorry," the cop added. "My sister went missing twenty years ago. I remember how frustrated I got when people couldn't or wouldn't help me."

"Did you find your sister?" The husband asked, his English barely understandable.

"Yes."

Price could tell they were both seeing what the memory was doing to him. Their anger and frustration was replaced by concern and maybe fear that in twenty years *their* pain would still be just below the surface.

"She was dead, wasn't she?"

The husband said that in Dari which fortunately Price understood.

"Yes," he replied in the same language.

"Please, you two, English," the woman muttered before looking at Charlie earnestly. "She was a good girl."

"She *is* a good girl," the man looked frustrated. "But she is also a teenager; an *American* teenager."

They spoke for another twenty minutes, the way Aliah's parents told their daughter's story made her sound like a typical 15 year old: She had friends, liked going out, did not have a boyfriend.

Good grades, rebellious on occasion. They had last seen her leaving for school.

"May I see her room?" Price asked.

The man and the woman looked at each other and discussed the matter in Dari. The mother looked at Price, still unsure.

"How would this help?" She asked.

"If she ran away—" Charlie replied.

"She was a good girl," the father said firmly, looking into Charlie's eyes.

"Her room will tell more about her than words can, do you understand?" The cop responded.

More discussion in Dari.

"Please do not spend too much time in there and do not touch anything," the woman said.

Price nodded and she led him down a hallway that smelled like cheap carpet cleaner. On one door in sparkly letters was the girl's name. The cop walked in, smelled clean laundry and some sort of inexpensive but girly perfume, a loud smell. On the walls were posters of attractive boys in groups that Charlie assumed were boy bands. The lettering on the posters was Asian, appeared Korean like the boys.

"She is crazy about those Korean bands," the mother sighed, leaning in the doorframe.

Charlie just nodded. There was something black snaking from beneath the bed, he knelt down to see what it was—a cable, a cable leading to a microphone. The cop started to pull out the microphone but there was an anxious voice from the doorway.

"Please, do not touch!"

Part of him wanted to remind the woman that he was investigating the disappearance of their daughter but part of him understood: They didn't want to disturb her room, if nothing changed then maybe Aliah would return and all of them could pretend like nothing happened.

"Did Aliah do music as a hobby?" He asked.

"*Do* music?"

"You know, some kids will have music software, make up songs and stuff..."

The mother's face changed, she was hiding something.

"Look...the odds of me finding Aliah get much better if I know everything," Price added.

The woman walked in, sat on the bed, and then jumped up and smoothed the comforter where she had briefly sat.

"She wanted to be a pop star," the mother said quietly. "She was a good girl...got good grades, did not spend time with bad kids...we felt that she deserved this, singing...get it out of her system."

"What did she do? Did she have a program like Garageband or something?"

"No. There is a local man, calls himself a record producer; for money he helps people come up with a song and makes a video for that song."

"How much did he charge you?"

"Ten thousand dollars."

Price didn't know how much a recording and video were supposed to cost but assumed a professional recording was expensive—if this was a professional deal and not some letch luring young girls into a darkened "recording studio."

"Do you have a copy of it you can play me?" He asked.

The mother looked stricken: *Please, I can't bear to listen to it now*...her eyes and face said that.

"It may help me figure out what's going on with Aliah," Charlie explained gently.

The woman just stared at him and then went to a pink laptop on the small, pink desk. She opened the computer and brought up the recording. Charlie closed his eyes and listened carefully: The music track was uninspired, a lot of presets both in the keyboards and drum machines and Aliah's voice was heavily auto-tuned. The recording sounded professional, however, like all the equipment was professional grade. The record producer was probably legit, but he'd still be worth interviewing.

"What do you think?" A small voice, a mother peeking in, leery but needing to know.

"It sounds like a professional recording," Charlie replied, holding back his opinion that Aliah couldn't sing, not that such a thing mattered in pop music. He looked over at her, the woman looked disappointed; she was probably hoping the music producer was a scam artist then he would be the most likely suspect and soon the case would be solved.

"We'll find her," Price forced a smile; it had to look as fake as it felt.

The mother forced a smile of her own and then showed her guest out of her missing daughter's room and the nondescript ranch house.

A fifteen year old Acura pulled up behind Charlie's Mercedes, bass rattling the deeply tinted windows; it had to be Aliah's older brother. The wheels looked expensive; were they a gift like the ten grand for Aliah's recording or was the young man working? If the latter, what did he do? The motor was silenced and in turn the stereo; no one emerged from the car. Price thought of Charlie Russell staring out of a Nissan Sentra, hateful, raising a revolver—

A young man emerged from the Acura: Around twenty. Hair and clothes stylish. Charlie could smell his cologne from fifteen feet away, it was covering the smell of sweat because everyone was sweating. The young man was arguing down a phone in another language, Spanish....Spanish even though he was Afghani. The call ended, Charlie saw an opening to a conversation and unlike in the past there was no hesitation—no hesitation or over thinking or concern.

"I'm Inspector Price from the police," Charlie said, taking a step towards the young man. "I'm guessing you're Aliah's brother."

"Yeah," dismissive, no concern, no *do you have any idea how to find my sister.*

"Do you have any ideas where she may have gone," the cop looked over at the house meaningfully and back at the kid. "Just between us, anything your sister may be doing that your parents don't know about."

"No, bro." The younger man was walking towards the house and away from the conversation.

"We need all the help we can get finding Aliah," Charlie pressed, following the young man down the walkway.

The Afghani stopped and turned back towards Price.

"It's your fucking job, bro. Why don't you just do it?" He looked up at the sun as if he hated it. "It's too fucking hot for talking."

The cop stopped, taken aback by the rudeness; the young man used Price's surprise to escape the conversation and walk into the house.

Mustache Man

There was a new abandoned car on his block: A ten to fifteen year old Kia sedan. Intact; that would change in hours. Parking in front of it was an even more antique Oldsmobile 88 that Charlie guessed was from the early 90s. A heavy man wearing aviator sunglasses with a white mustache was leaning against the right side of the trunk and smoking, his forehead shiny with sweat. Price put him somewhere in his early sixties—there was something familiar about the car and the man and it bothered him that he couldn't make a connection. Hefty Smoker was looking right at him. Charlie parked in front of his house and walked over to the stranger.

"Nice night, huh?" The man nodded, tapping his ash into the street.

"Yeah, certainly better than they predicted."

The stranger took one last drag and flicked the butt into the gutter, the cop was too distracted for it to register.

"You're a plainclothes cop, right?" the man asked, pulling a tissue from his pocket and dabbing the sweat off his forehead, leaving a couple of tiny fragments of wet tissue behind.

The heat had slowed Charlie's response; it wasn't a strange question, lots of people in the neighborhood knew that he was a cop.

"Yeah, an Inspector."

The stranger nodded, got out his pack, put a cigarette in his mouth, and lit it with a black disposable lighter.

"Do you remember being a patrolman?" He asked.

That was an usual question but—

Charlie realized that he *didn't* have any recollections of being a uniform, had no memories of seeing himself in the mirror dressed in his blues or anything like that.

"I am taking from your expression that you have no memories of being a patrolman," the smoker continued.

Price didn't answer—what was the man's agenda?

And why *didn't* he remember being a patrolman? All cops had to start as patrolmen, right?

"I was in the military," Charlie said firmly, not wanting to share his doubt with the stranger. "An officer...the police department had an officer's program for people like me."

That answer came easily, maybe it was the right one—

It's the bullet to the head, that's all.

Really? Then why were his instincts telling him that it was more than that. The stranger took a long drag, tilted his head and seemed to appraise Price.

"We're just running down the clock, Inspector."

He smiled a thin lip smile, flicked a second cigarette in the gutter, and walked around to the driver's side. Charlie watched him drive off.

The Fat Chance

Charlie wanted to dig through his records, find the file on his employment with the precinct, but there was a missing girl to contend with; missing girls had to be found quickly before they became dead girls...or girls sold off as sex slaves in some foreign country or something horrific like that.

We're just running down the clock...

No. Focus—-Aliah's life depends on it.

The brother was suspicious, how uncaring he seemed, but grief brings out different reactions in different people; Celeste going missing had proven that. Charlie had been distraught while his mother had seemed angry---he knew her well enough it was her way of keeping it together by choosing anger over hopeless grief...

Do you remember being a patrolman?

No, he wouldn't let that distract him, the question may circle around and around in his mind but he wouldn't let it distract him.

It was just regulars at the Fat Chance and the smell of hot mold coming from the swamp cooler. One of the barflies had a brackish cough that reminded Price of tuberculosis. Thinking of TB made him think of what that disease had been called in the old days, consumption—

This led to his memory dreams of the past—

I was shot in the head; those dreams of being a soldier in the 1800s were just a coma dream.

Are you sure? They seemed more like memories than dreams and—

Stop. Just...STOP.

"What's on your mind, captain?" Chris had come over; the cop hadn't noticed.

"We're just running down the clock," Charlie mumbled.

"Yes, well, we *are* in a bar…"

"People keep saying that to me; a kid being booked, some older dude with a mustache near my house."

"This is real, not a dream," Price continued. "I'm not imagining it."

Chris focused on wiping the bar in front of Price in tight circles.

"You need to see someone, dude," he said eventually. "Your doctor…you need to make an appointment because this could be a sign that not all the damage in your brain was taken care of."

"You think it's a hallucination?"

The bartender stopped wiping, looked up at his friend.

"You have two different people saying the same thing; think about that. Also, the guy with the mustache…Oldsmobile from thirty years ago, right?"

"Yeah—"

"You mentioned him shortly before you got shot, he was dumping trash next to an abandoned car."

The memory came back; Charlie decided not to tell Chris about the question regarding his being a patrolman, his friend would probably just get more concerned.

"Maybe you're right,"the cop sighed. "I'll make an appointment with my doctor tomorrow."

The bartender smiled at that.

"You're gonna be okay, dude, you seem good other than the hallucinations."

One of the barflies bawled about a new drink, Chris went down to help him and then returned to Charlie.

"So, you back on duty?"

"Yeah, already got a missing persons case."

"Missing persons? I didn't know you handled those, thought you were burglary."

"It's because the family is Afghani."

"And you speak Pashto..."Chris nodded in understanding.

"This family speaks Dari, but whomever started the file just registered that they're *Afghani*, I guess."

The lights flickered, the bartender stopped wiping and scowled up at them.

"It would be a miracle if they even knew about Pashto," he said after looking back at his friend.

"Maybe it was one of the uniforms that had been on the service."

The lights flickered again, a few people in the bar groaned.

"The swamp cooler takes a lot of juice," the bartender explained to the room. "You want me to shut it off?"

There were a few responses in the negative.

"Well, then," the bartender added. "In that case shut your holes."

Price walked home. It was twilight so the heat was manageable. The orange cat was sitting in the backyard, looking up at a tree as if watching a bird and then over at Charlie's kitchen window as the cop looked out it. The cat's mouth was moving, it was talking to him—wanting food? Wanting to be let in? Something else? The cop was distracted by a headache that came on quickly; as he rarely got headache the sensation gave him anxiety:

Chris was right, there could be some damage there, a broken blood vessel or something...what if I decided too late to see a doctor?

Desperate, he went to the piano in the hope that playing would recenter him; it hurt too much to sit up so he went into the bedroom, lay down, and closed his eyes.

He was on a side street at night in a bad part of town. Charlie heard a muffled bass signature, a car was rolling up. Turning, he saw it was a beat up Nissan Sentra, *the* Nissan Sentra. Knowing what was to come, Price considered running off but found he couldn't move. The music was silenced, the front passenger window came down. It was Charlie Russell.

"This is how it really goes, motherfucker," the child said with a scowl.

He leveled a revolver at the cop and it blew up, destroying half his face and spraying blood all over the driver who just stared ahead and nodded her head as if to music Price couldn't hear. The boy with the gun didn't scream but his mouth dropped open as if unhinged and he began to convulse---

The Doctor

The headache was gone when Charlie woke up. It was early but already the heat was persistent; the cop could feel it coming through the nearest wall. The news website claimed it was going to be 118 that day. After a cup of coffee, he called the medical centre and they were able to get Price in that afternoon; the urgency and the tone of the nurse's voice didn't sit well with the cop.

This is bad; my hallucinations or whatever they are indicate something wrong, irreputable brain damage or something.

And what about the headache the night before? He *never* got headaches. The dream...was the boy's head being destroyed symbolic of the headache?

No, that's what really happened—

No...I was shot in the head by Charlie Russell....

The cop walked to the bathroom and turned on the light. He examined the upper reaches of his forehead until he found the scar—(nearly invisible, they had done a good job)—and the dent in his skin which was covering the hole in his skull where the bullet had entered. That cured some of his anxiety, but there was still the issue of the hallucinations.

Fifteen minutes before his appointment, Charlie parked in the garage next to the medical centre. The old Mercedes seemed to be relieved to be out of the direct sunlight where it had struggled not to overheat at the traffic lights. The cop had no choice but to keep the air conditioning on the lowest setting and the back of his shirt had become wet, trapped against the vinyl seatback. He locked the car, walked into the building, and found the doctor's office. The waiting room was empty. He sat in the chair directly across from the receptionist and toyed with his phone until his name was called. The nurse was a Black woman, thin and very businesslike, who asked about his symptoms and seemed bothered by what he told her; she tried to conceal it but failed. Ten minutes after she left, an Arab looking man in a white coat entered, smiling warmly at the cop.

Not Arab...Afghani.

That confused Charlie; his doctor in the hospital had been a black man in his late fifties with a habit of frowning whenever answering the patient's questions.

"Good afternoon, Charlie," the man in the white coat smiled, pulling a chair next to the exam table. "So...you are having some recovery symptoms that are troubling you?"

"I'm sorry...what happened to Dr. Fillmore?"

"Dr. Fillmore?" The doctor sat back a little, looked confused. "My name is Dr. Yebulla—don't you remember?"

"The doctor I had at the hospital, his name was Fillmore."

Dr. Yebulla looked concerned and his open concern brought Charlie's anxiety back: *Don't be an idiot; Dr. Fillmore probably only works in the hospital. There are so many doctors and nurses that this doctor simply is not familiar with every other doctor.*

"Charlie...I am your doctor," Yebulla said softly. "I was the one who performed surgery, well, one of the doctors."

"Please, do not be scared," he continued, sitting forward again, forcing a smile but failing to have one in his eyes. "I am sure there is an explanation."

He asked Price about his equilibrium, motor skills, and then asked about any pain.

"Yeah, I had a really bad headache last night."

Dr. Yebulla frowned at that.

"Where was the pain centered?"

It had been where the scar was; Charlie reluctantly shared that.

They're gonna have to open me up again, I know it.

Dr. Yebulla sat back again, making notes in a tablet he had pulled from a coat pocket.

"Tell me more about these hallucinations."

"They were more like *dreams*. Vivid ones that didn't feel like dreams..."

And this is where I sound like a crazy person...or someone with permanent brain damage...

Price had to remind himself that this man, this doctor, was not connected to the police; whatever he told Yebulla would not go on his record.

"I was shot at by these kids and it traumatized me, not being shot at, my fear was that I couldn't save them. I started having memories and they felt real of me being a British soldier in the 1800s. I went to see a therapist and she explained that I had a rare genetic condition and had been born in the 1600s. And then I was this hermit living in the desert, hiding out because I had killed a bunch of people to avenge this woman I loved....see, it's all just *crazy*."

The doctor smiled and chuckled, this time the smile was clearly genuine.

"Charlie...you were in a coma, I have heard of a wide variety of dreams, very vivid dreams, in the coma state. Sometimes there are no dreams, sometimes there are, there are no rules."

"Does it depend on where you get shot in the brain?"

"You know," Yebulla replied thoughtfully. "I have never thought about that."

He sat forward again, focusing on Charlie with a serious expression.

"You have good motor skills and reflexes. Your speech is good, eye movement...the only thing that concerns me is that headache last night. But..."

He sighed, sat back, looked at the ceiling for a moment then at Charlie.

"There is so little we know about the brain. The reality is, a bullet struck your brain, the damage was not fatal, it was healing normally when we closed you up, but you are bound to experience things you have not experienced before because the structure of your brain has changed."

He watched the patient's reaction carefully and then smile what appeared to be a genuinely kind smile.

"I know that sounds dramatic, but it is not necessarily a bad thing; do not be concerned...please."

"Okay."

Dr. Yebulla stood up and put the chair back where he had gotten it.

"Remember, Charlie; we're only running down the clock," he said with his back to the cop.

"Drink lots of water," he turned towards his patient with a different smile, one the cop couldn't place. "It is supposed to be 116 today."

Hot Tip

Aliah had recorded the song and the video through something called Hot Tip Productions. Charlie looked up the number and started to dial it—

Where's the hesitation? Where's the anxiety about a phone call, the preparation for the conversation?

He was calm...and the irony was that the feelings of calmness gave him anxiety, the calmness felt like an alien that was taking over his mind.

Just relax; maybe this is a plus side of being shot in the head.

A man answered the phone. Charlie explained who he was and asked if the man had fifteen minutes to talk to him.

"What do you want with me, officer?" Suspicion, maybe some anger.

"We have a missing girl, she recently worked with your production company."

"You need to be more specific," less confusion, more impatience than anything.

"Her name is Aliah, Afghani teenager."

"I remember an Aliah. Afghani? I thought she was Arab or something..."

"Do you have fifteen minutes, sir?"

"Can we do this over the phone?"

"Sorry, it needs to be in person."

The man on the other end sighed.

"Can you come by at three o' clock?"

The address was in a newer, gated community: Large houses in various earth tones. Tiny lots. Fledgling trees on stakes that the heat was testing. The newer Dodge Charger in the driveway was immaculately polished; the ruthless sun made the chrome wink like it was in on the joke. There were no license plates on the black sedan; it bothered the cop but he had more important business than a lack of proper registration. Charlie parked out front and walked up a cement ribbon to the front door. Again, there was no anxiety, no need to prepare for the conversation. The man who answered the door was Black, anywhere between late twenties and late thirties. Bald head with a carefully shaped stubble beard. Muscular, a few inches taller than the cop. Expensive looking polo shirt, jeans, loafers, and cologne that reminded the cop of teak.

"You must be Inspector Price," he extended a hand, smiling like a manager about to reprimand an underling.

"Yes—"

"You should come in the foyer, I don't want to let the air conditioning out."

He looked the cop over and Price felt subconscious about his sweaty face and clothes as he followed the producer into the entry. It was spotless and tidy, the tile was light beige and without a single scuff or trace of dirt, Charlie could feel the coolness of it beneath his shoes.

"I had a session run late so I've got ten minutes max," the producer continued. "Can we do this here?"

"Yes," Price pulled out his phone, dropped into an app, and started recording.

"First, let me get some background: What is your title and how long have you been doing it?" He asked.

"I am a music producer and video director. How long? Ah, ten years."

"And have you always worked with unknowns like Aliah?"

The producer had to think about that one.

"Well—have you heard of Low2Dipz?"

"The name is familiar."

"I worked with him four or five years ago," he frowned. "We had a verbal agreement...that was a real lesson."

"What happened?"

"I was supposed to be his partner, the one making tracks for him, but he got a new manager and the manager elbowed me out."

"It's a rough business, isn't it?"

"Um, hmm," the producer said curtly. "But you are here about a missing girl..."

"How did you come to know Aliah?" He asked.

The producer pulled out his own phone and consulted it.

"April 15th. Her mother contacted me as legal guardian. Aliah had heard about Hot Tip, wanted to do a song and video...she had heard of the special promotion I do: $10000 for one track and a video."

"And this is the way prospective entertainers contact you?"

"Prospective entertainers," the producer repeated, smirking and then covering it up. "It varies. With teens like Aliah with no experience in the business, yeah, they hear about Hot Tip over social media. With people in the business maybe they hear it from an engineer or a musician."

Charlie studied the producer for a couple of months, attempting to read him, trying to unseat him with scrutiny. As before, he was surprised that eye contact didn't make him uncomfortable. The producer stared back; either he wasn't hiding anything or he had missed his calling as an actor.

"What was your impression of Aliah when you met her?"

"As a singer or a girl?"

"Let's start with as a girl..."

"Just an ordinary teenage girl," the producer shrugged. "Cute, but like a hundred cute girls at any mall."

Cute? Did that mean he was attracted to Aliah which could take the investigation in another direction? No, her cuteness was just a detail to the producer, Charlie could see that on his face.

"What about as a singer?" He asked.

"Not good but not the worst I've heard. I'm a miracle man, bro, I can use Pro Tools, auto tune...I can fix even a terrible voice. It's what the pros do."

He looked down at his phone.

"We need to wrap this up; we're running down the clock."

"Did you know she disappeared?" Charlie asked.

The producer looked back, nothing changed in his eyes or his expression.

"Doesn't surprise me."

"Why do you say that?"

"That girl wanted to escape," the producer said levelly. "She was bored with the life of a normal, American teenager, she put everything on the work I did for her, all her hopes and dreams of getting away from her school, her family, this ordinary life. I didn't see much of a future for her in music; for girls like her these sessions end up being a distraction then a disappointment then a fond memory, the first and last hopefully the longest in duration."

He looked down at his phone again.

"And now I've got to say good day, sir. If you have any further questions, call to make an appointment."

"Thank you for your time."

The cop was barely out the door when it closed behind him. The chrome on the car seemed to be winking even more fiercely like it knew something and took pleasure understanding Charlie would never figure it out.

The Favor

"Are you asking as Inspector Price or my friend Charlie?" Chris, leaning across the bar, looking wary.

He was wearing a t-shirt with Elvis Costello's face on, the design was faded and the shirt was transparent in places from sweat. Holes were starting next to the bottom hem.

"I wouldn't ask as Inspector Price," Charlie was clutching his glass of tonic water, enjoying the coolness of it in his hand.

The bartender glanced around to make sure no one was close enough to hear their conversation.

"I know someone," the bartender confirmed. "You want me to send them your way?"

"Yes, thanks."

Chris went back in the kitchen and returned with a plate of nachos for one of the tables.

"I wish we could stop serving food during this heatwave," he grumbled to Charlie before taking the plate to one of the tables. The lights flickered and continued to flicker for what felt like twenty seconds. Price watched them—what *if* the power went out? How long could people survive without air conditioning and fridges to keep their ice water and soda and beer cold. How long would the human race endure without power to make nachos?

"Is this for something personal or work?" Chris had returned and was leaning across the bar, his shirt so sweated through you could see his chest hair.

"Work."

"And there isn't someone there who can do the job?"

"Not legally, right to privacy and all that."

Someone leaned on the other end of the bar, looking over at Chris and meaningfully and tapping the wood with an empty bottle. The bartender held up an index finger to silence him and continued to focus on his friend.

"Aren't you worried about being found out and losing your job?" Charlie wasn't, he didn't really care. It wasn't *not caring* in a nihilistic way, it was not caring in that he couldn't be bothered to be worried.

"No. I mean, they could fire me if they found out, but this situation is too important and time sensitive to deal with red tape."

"Not to be nosy, but—"

"It's the missing girl. I'm hoping your friend can get me into her social media, Google docs...anything to get a lead."

"Family hasn't been of any use?"

"No. This guy I'm assuming is the brother is the worst," Charlie took a long drink from his glass. "You think he'd be all over me to find his little sister, doing whatever to help, being a pest...no, just the opposite. He was a real punk."

The guy at the end of the bar was now glaring at Chris and waving the empty bottle over his head.

"Duty calls," Chris rolled his eyes as he said that.

Hacker

Charlie had gotten it down to 85 in the house but there had been a burning plastic smell and the lights had flickered so the cop had, reluctantly, dialed the air conditioning back. When refilling his water glass, he had seen the orange cat through the window. Price went to the back door. He rarely opened it so the locks were frozen; he sprayed cooking spray on the clasps and got them to release. Opening the door reminded him of when you stick your face in the oven to check if your food is done.

"You want to come in?" He asked the cat from twenty feet away. "Choose quickly cause it's brutal out here."

The cat looked at him for a few seconds then walked off. Before Price could close the door, he heard a motorcycle engine, it seemed to cut out in front of the house. Curious, he walked to the front window. Someone was working to get a helmet off, a woman, he could tell by the breasts that were pushing through a sweaty green sleeveless tee. She was somewhere in her thirties with spiky black hair, a sharp nose, and aviator sunglasses. He had the door open before she reached it; she was a stranger but his intuition told him that she was not meant to continue being a stranger. They walked into the living room.

"Can I get you any water?"

"Water?" She frowned. "Do you have any beer?"

"No, sorry—"

"This is beer weather," she replied. "I don't know how people can drink coffee."

The woman looked over at him intently, Charlie was struggling not to stare at her breasts through the transparent shirt.

"I saw that in a restaurant where I was picking up lunch," the stranger continued. "Dude ordered a cup of coffee, you could see the steam coming off it. Why?"

"I don't know—"

"You have no idea who I am," she said quietly, walking to the piano and sitting at the bench, playing a couple of chords. "Your friend told me you need help with a computer. Is this place clean?"

"Clean?"

"Have you checked for mics? You are a cop but I can't tell if you are a paranoid cop."

"Why would they put mics in my house?"

The woman got up from the bench and pulled a small phone from the back pocket of her jeans, she poked at it, held it up and did a slow 360, and looked at the screen.

"It is clean," she said. "You look like you need a name..."

"No, I mean, if that's not normal in this situation—"

"You can call me Marika if you need a name," the woman sat back on the piano bench and appeared to be studying him. "So...you need me to open some doors and windows?"

It took a couple of moments for Charlie to figure out what she meant.

"Yes."

"Write down what you know about her on a piece of paper."

"You're not worried about a paper trail?"

"There's a lot more danger if you text or email it, believe me. Paper can be destroyed, digital stuff...there are always ghosts."

He could smell her sweat; it was a logical smell seeing as he had ridden there on a motorcycle. How did she stand it, riding a bike, not protection from the sun? *Marika*. She took the paper when he was done with it and frowned at what she saw.

"This girl, she is teenaged---you are not a pedo or something are you?"

"No, it has to do with a case."

That made sense to Marika, you could tell by the expression on her face.

"And you wanted to avoid the red tape? Very smart."

"How much will this cost?"

"Fifty an hour, but it shouldn't take me much more than an hour to get in. Teenagers...not the best at coming up with uncrackable passwords."

Marika got up from the bench and knelt down to get her helmet.

"Are you going to jerk off after I leave?" She asked at the door.

"What?"

"You kept looking at my tits, I was just curious."

Charlie had no response to that, Marika smirked and walked back into the heat.

Meeting With The Boss

Charlie slept in the living room after pulling his sheet off the bed and draping it over the couch. According to the news, the power grid was severely overloaded and there would be rolling blackouts over the next few days. At the bottom of the report was a list of cooling centers in the city where people with no power could go for air conditioning. It didn't get below 90 that night, thirty degrees above normal for that time of year.

When the cop woke up, he saw that he had gotten a text from the captain asking him to come in at ten and give him an update on the missing girl case.

"Please be prompt," the text ended. "I have fifteen other inspectors to meet with today."

Picking out his clothes, he saw his favorite slacks in the dirty clothes basket and pulled them out—they had been mended, *why*? His intuition told him that the memory was important but the memory was elusive.

Come on...you got shot in the head, it's no mystery why you can't remember. It was probably something innocuous, stop being a neurotic mess.

Price drove to work with his window and the right rear one down; those were the only two power windows that still worked in the old Mercedes. He didn't dare switch the air conditioner on as the temp gauge was already at the three quarter mark. He had started off wearing a sport coat but it was too hot, let the Captain discipline him if he wanted.

"Hey, buddy!" Captain exclaimed when Price walked in.

His boss was smiling but didn't look up from his laptop, probably refreshing his memory as to what "Ten o' clock" was supposed to be working on. Price stood ten feet from the desk, the Captain motioned to a chair and the inspector sat in it. His boss was also in shirtsleeves, although it was comfortable in his office, probably only mid-seventies.

"So," Captain looked over at Charlie. "What do we have on the missing girl?"

"Not much, yet. The only thing of interest was that she recorded a song and a video so I visited the producer—"

"Yeah, yeah, I read that in your update. What do you have to go on from here?"

"Friends. She had a few, hopefully one or two of them will open up."

"Good, good," the Captain winked, looking down at his laptop then closing it dramatically. "You staying cool, inspector?"

"Trying, Captain."

His boss looked thoughtful, the smile on his face disappearing.

"This girl is crucial, Price. This is why we put you, a key player on the team, on it."

I thought it was because I speak an Afghani language...even if it's the wrong one.

"The work near the mosque," Captain frowned. "It has been putting the Arab community...wait, Arab? Muslim?"

"Muslim, captain. Arabs are a type of Muslim."

"What are the girl's people, are they Arab?"

"Afghani."

The Captain nodded as if he understood, he probably didn't.

"We need to find this girl, inspector, show the Muslim community that we care, that they're important."

He opened his laptop and brought up something, probably his next appointment.

"I'm guessing they're enjoying this heat," he added.

"Captain?"

"Reminds them of home, I'd imagine." The boss mused before looking up with a big smile.

"Thanks for bringing me up to speed, boss," he added.

"Appreciate you."

The Captain looked back down at his laptop. Understanding that was his cue to leave, Charlie stood up and walked out of the office.

The Boondocks

A text from Dawn: "Meet me in the Boondocks." The
Boondocks was the attic, a disused part of the station; you needed
a special key to even get in there, a skeleton key, at that—
What did she want? Talk about their situation? Maybe confess
that she wanted to run away with—
Don't be a fucking idiot.
Charlie had only been to the Boondocks a couple of times, once
when he was new to the precinct---a variety of hazing. The door
to the stairs was in the back of a utility closet, the cop
remembered that much. He had to investigate two utility closets
before finding the right one. Past the last shelf of musty looking
cardboard boxes was an interior door that appeared over a
hundred years old complete with a glass doorknob; Price turned it
and the door opened to a short vestibule and then a steep, narrow
staircase that smelled of old plaster. Dawn had switched the light
on. On the wall to Charlie's left was a charcoal drawing of a
man's face with an enormous broom of a mustache. Written
below the drawing was: "GF—OUR PATRON SAINT." At the
top of the stairs it opened into a narrow but long room with a six
foot ceiling. Price expected it to be unbearably hot up
there—there weren't ventilation ducts to the Boondocks—but
Dawn had set a portable air conditioner on a dusty chair giving
there a few square feet of bearable space. Mendez was waiting for
him, smiling slightly when he emerged. What was he supposed to
do? Embrace her? No, he had no idea of her intention. Charlie
walked over until he was three or four feet from his partner.
"The world is burning up," she said.

He just looked at her for a few moments, struggling with his feelings. The words normally came easy with her but this was not a normal situation, not at all.

"It feels like it."

"We can never go back," she said, her smile replaced with a sad expression.

"Pardon?" But he thought he understood—*we can never go back to when I visited you.*

"I get it," he added a second later.

"No, I doubt you do," Dawn said. "I just want you to know that I think about it, what happened but....as much as I care about you, I love my family more."

She looked down.

"You keep pulling me in, you know?" Mendez added.

"I don't—"

"I feel it all the time," his partner continued. "I have to be strong, though."

He had no idea what to say. She was making the right choice but he hadn't wanted her to make the right choice

"You shouldn't have gotten in the truck," Dawn said softly, barely audible.

"What?"

"You'll understand at some point," she said, reaching down to switch off the air conditioner. "I brought it up; you can take it down."

He just nodded. She touched his lips with her right index finger but gave him a wide berth as she walked to the stairs and out of sight.

You shouldn't have gotten in the truck.

Fifty Dollars Cash

It was 118 degrees by four in the afternoon. Crows were in the shade, panting, some of the corvids—and other birds—had fallen out of the trees dead. It was 92 in Charlie's house and they were predicting 121 the following day. The cop had watched a video of the weather cast; the metrologist had a sweaty face and looking tired as well as frightened.

"So, we're looking at 121 tomorrow, the old record for that day of the year was 93," he looked off camera and chuckled nervously. "Anyone know if we've jumped our orbit and are headed towards the sun?"

No one returned his laughter; hearing the sound of a motorcycle out front, Price closed the video and his laptop. The computer was hot, he made a mental note to put it in the fridge to cool it down—the fridge, it was always running, struggling—how long until it broke down? How long until the air conditioner, which was now making a rattling noise, quit? He went to the front door before Marika knocked and opened it at the last second. She was wearing a tank top and long, khaki shorts with a bulge going down one leg as if she had a large penis.

"Jesus, it's not much better in here," the hacker said with a scowl. "The air conditioner smells like burning plastic if I turn it up."

Marika shrugged and dropped onto the couch.

"So...I got into the girl's social media, email....all the same password. It took me five minutes but I have a one hour minimum."

"Wow...that was fast."

"I was a teenage girl once," She shrugged before fishing around in a pocket and withdrawing a piece of paper that she handed to Charlie.

"Do you want cash or do you have a PayPal or something?"

"Do you have fifty in cash?"

Price had gotten cash that morning and handed sixty dollars over.

"Keep the change."

"I was going to."

The hacker pulled a beer out of the bulging pocket and twisted the top off. The suspicious bump in her shorts was gone and the cop couldn't decide if he was disappointed or not.

"Your drinking must have been bad to quit," she said after a long swallow.

"It was."

Marika looked over at the piano.

"Were you ever a musician or something?" Charlie asked.

She looked over at him warily.

"I just wondered because you seem drawn to the piano," the cop added.

The hacker focused on peeling the label for a few seconds before looking back at Price.

"Yeah, I used to have a band, all in the past."

She took a drink of her beer.

"I do not go into things I access normally," Marika continued.

"But, I heard the song this girl did...."

The hacker took a long drink, the bottle was nearly empty.

"Fucking awful," she sighed.

"She isn't much of a singer," Charlie agreed then felt weird criticizing someone who may have died.

"It's not just the singing," the woman on the couch clarified. "There's no soul to it, the whole thing, it's all cut and pasted and processed...cold. Clinical. It's funny, the girl must have had this passion to transcend her life but there's no passion in her singing, there is as much life to her performance as there is in a pet that has been left in a hot car."

Marika finished her beer.

"I need to go home and take a cold shower, anything to beat this heat."

She walked to the front door and then stopped and looked back at Price.

"I think she's gone, Inspector. I think you've understood you wouldn't find her from the beginning."

"I can't think that way."

The hacker looked thoughtful, he could smell her sweat.

"You have to let it go or you will keep coming back here."

Before Charlie could ask for clarification, the hacker walked out the front door.

Top Krew

Charlie sat on the hacked information overnight, guilty about the invasion of privacy...

Reluctantly, he went in the following morning. Aliah's MeMeMe page revealed little to the cop at first, there were a lot of memes she had borrowed from others, links to news about Korean boy bands she followed—

A series of flat stones skipping over a shallow body of water. Aliah had quite a few likes but few comments. Charlie studied her *Top Krew*, her "closet friends" on the social media platform; it was four teenaged girls, three white and one Hispanic in appearance. He needed to interview them, see if they had an idea where Aliah may have gone to—

Kidnapped. You need to admit to yourself she was kidnapped; Aliah is either far away or dead...like Celeste.

Stop. Just...stop.

The girls were probably at a cooling station seeing as the rolling blackouts were ending private air conditioning and refrigerators along with outlets to charge phones and other devices. They were predicting 124 that day—how was that even possible? Price didn't want to imagine how hot it would be in places like Phoenix or El Paso.

Aliah rarely used email. Most of the action on her account was messages from her parents that she responded to or spam. The texts on her phone were almost exclusively from her "Top Krew" with a handful coming from the music producer Charlie had interviewed. The texts between him and the girl revealed little: Confirming appointments and that one of her parents were be present. Directions to his house. Still logged into Aliah's

MeMeMe, Charlie sent a message to a girl named Givenchy. He contemplated explaining that he was a cop but remembering how he had accessed the account reconsidered that idea.

"How are you?" He wrote.

The message was immediately read.

"WTF?" Was Givenchy's response. "Where U been? Heard you got kidnapped by some China bro-z or something crazy like that."

"I'm heading to the cooling shelter on Burnside. Are you there?"

"Yeah. Where else would we be?"

The cooling shelter on Burnside was a mile away. Charlie hoped he could drive the distance before the car overheated. At ten in the morning it was already 109 degrees. Dead birds were on the sidewalks and grassy areas he passed. He could feel the sun's harshness through the windows and the roof of the old Mercedes. No one was on the street, vehicles were on the side of the road; not parked, the way they were situated it was clear they had succumbed to the heat. Price's car was running rough, shaking as it idled at red lights.

The parking lot of the cooling shelter was nearly full. It had been a two story department store back in the days that department stores could thrive, Charlie recalled going there to buy his favorite slacks several years earlier. Price parked and locked up his car. The heat was immediately in his lungs, it was like breathing steam. He considered himself to be in good shape but the two or three hundred feet to the doors nearly made him swoon. The glass entry doors had been insulated by what looked like moving blankets.

COOLING SHELTER: PLEASE MAKE SURE DOOR IS CLOSED BEHIND YOU

The handle was as hot as an oven rack. After jerking his hand back in surprise and pain, Charlie used the bottom of his shirt to grasp the handle. Inside the building was a woman sitting at a folding table that had a couple dozen labeless bottles of water on it.

"We should have added a warning to the sign," she frowned.

"Pardon?"

"For the door handle, how hot it is."

"I should have assumed it, seeing how it is 109 degrees."

She smiled at that.

"We have plenty of water if you need it."

"Thanks—"

"One lady saw the ones on this table and got anxious; I had to reassure her that there is more in the back, these ones are simply representative of the total number of bottles of water we have."

"I understand—"

"Oh, and F.Y.I. we've blocked off the second floor; trying to control the heat up there uses too much power."

"Okay, thanks."

It had to be in the low eighties where they were, Charlie guessed that where the people were taking refuge in mass it would be even warmer. He had expected a large room full of cots with dejected people sitting on them and luggage shoved underneath but instead came across a warren of small cubicles, each one with three cots. There was the sound of dozens of conversations, some loud voices and some moderate, the cubicles muffed a lot of the sound, he assumed—how was he even going to find Givenchy? The cop pulled out his phone and accessed Aliah's MeMeMe again.

"I'm here—where are you?" He messaged the girl.

"Off to the right after you walk in, some bro put up an American flag for some reason, we're behind it."

Price followed the instruction, bracing himself for the negative reaction when he revealed his deception. He saw the flag, it was the size of a beach towel and pinned to the fabric wall of one of the cubicles. Givenchy was sitting on a cot in the cubie across the way with two other girls on the other cots, presumably the rest of Aliah's Top Krew. The teen didn't register the man standing in the opening to the cubicle. When Charlie said her name, she looked confused and maybe a bit creeped out that a strange man knew her name.

"I'm a cop, Givenchy. Sorry to deceive you but I am trying to find Aliah."

"Wait...that was you?" Now she looked even more uncomfortable.

"Don't talk to him," one of the other girls said loudly, looking sharply at Price. "He's a creep."

"No, I am a police inspector," Charlie pulled out his badge.

"How did you get on Aliah's MeMeMe?" Givenchy asked.

"He hacked her!" The other girl said accusingly.

"I am desperate to find her," Price responded, trying to figure out the best approach on his feet. "If we don't find missing girls quickly it usually ends up bad."

He saw Givenchy softening, walls coming down at little. The other girl was just staring at him hatefully.

"It's probably the Chinese bro-z," she said dismissively. "They've been buying girls."

"Chinese bro-z...where do they take the girls?"

The girl shrugged.

"It's supposed to be a decent life," she continued. "They take them to some big Asian city, buy them stuff, give them good food and all that. Nightlife...fun."

"Do you know how I could get ahold of these Chinese...bro-z?"

She looked at him as if he were an idiot for a moment before softening, appearing sad.

"It's too hot, Inspector Price," the girl said quietly, the anger gone from her face. "None of the phones work so we're all lost."

"Excuse me?"

"The phones," she said sadly. "They're too hot."

He pulled out his own phone, it *was* surprisingly hot.

The Hospital

People talking:
Temp is back to normal, I imagine he'll be regaining consciousness soon.
Could there be brain damage from the high body temp?
Don't know...hold on, it looks like he's regaining consciousness.
Two women were looking down at him, curious, medical outfits...nurses. Trying to make words, only a rasp coming, one of the women shaking her head. She was Black, somewhere in her forties, serious looking.
"Don't try to talk."
The other nurse was Black, late twenties, heavy set with a big mole on the left side of her neck. Was it a mole or a birthmark? She looked surprised, stunned as if she had just witnessed something dramatic like a nude man running out of a drug store.
"You're in a hospital," the older nurse smiled, but it was a tight, guarded smile. "You were found three days ago sitting in your truck."
"You nearly cooked," the younger nurse nodded and her companion gave her a sharp look.
The younger nurse looked contrite, took a step back; her name tag read Givenchy.
"Just relax," the older nurse smiled her thin line smile at Charlie again.
Still weak, Price did as he was told. Soon he slept; there were no dreams.

He had passed out in his truck next to the cabin. One of the miners on the ridge had seen him get in the truck. Coming back an hour later, he saw an unmoving man shape in the truck and went down to investigate. Charlie had been unconscious, an ambulance had been called that rushed him to Parumphp and then Las Vegas. As the days passed and he recovered further, Price remembered getting into his truck and thinking of Celeste—*why* he had, essentially, attempted suicide was unknown to him. The heat wave had clearly been a dream brought on by *cooking*—to quote the younger nurse—inside his truck. But the case about the missing girl—

And being shot in the head?

Charlie got up and walked to the bathroom to check his hairline; there was no indication of a bullet wound or the surgery to fix said wound.

So...Charlie Russell must have had the gun blow up in his face after all?

There was a red mark high on his forehead—*maybe* it was the entry point of a bullet?

What was the past? Had the angry child shot him? Or, after a long period of vengeance over his dead sister had he retreated to the desert to lie low?

Wait...what about the dream, (if it *was* a dream), of having lived four hundred years?

He was still looking in the mirror, his beard was unkempt and more than half gray by that point. Price ran a hand through it; he would shave it off after he was fully recovered.

His phone was in his pants pocket where he always kept it. Would Chris know anything? If he was having all these issues with his memory, had he already bothered his friend too much about them? Whether or not he had, Charlie knew he had to get to the bottom of things, his sanity depended on it.

"When you can talk, let me know," he texted the bartender.

"Only have three regulars right now—what's up?"

The ex cop(?) explained about how he had suffered heat stroke and while unconscious had a dream(?) about recovering from a gunshot wound to the head and trying to find a girl named Aliah. He went further back, about the possible timeline of his hiding out in the desert after avenging the death of his sister.

Chris didn't text back for the longest time.

"Can I call you?"

Price wasn't sure how his voice would hold up.

"Okay."

The phone rang in the middle of his processing that concern.

"What has got you thinking about her again?" Chris asked.

"Celeste?"

"Kind of," the bartender sighed. "Aliah."

"So...she was real, that was a real case of mine?"

"Yeah."

A question was forming in the cop's head, one he dreaded the answer to.

"I never found her, did I?"

Someone yelling in the background, the bartender holding the phone away from his face and yelling "Hold on, you fucking lush."

"No, dude," he continued gently down the phone. "And you kind of lost your shit—that was why you went out to the wastelands; you had a toasty and had to leave everything."

"So...I *wasn't* shot in the head."

"What?"

"It was either I got shot in the head or a boy tried to shoot me and the gun blew up in his face."

"Charlie Russell," Chris sighed. "Yeah, that didn't help things. You probably imagined getting shot because you would have preferred that to that stupid kid dying...especially after all you went through to save him and his friend."

"So, I didn't hide in the desert after avenging my sister's death? You know, there was also a dream or memory about being—"

"Immortal, yeah...that was when I knew you were in trouble, Captain."

"I am so confused right now..."

A long pause and then the bartender sighed.

"Charlie...you acted normal for a long time but I don't think you ever got over us finding Celeste. I think you understood that you would never find Aliah, that she would end up dead like Celeste—"

"But I never found her—"

"Charlie it's been over a year: She's dead, dude. Not to toss you deeper into the bell jar, but you need to accept that and move on."

"I think I have a new lead."

A long pause.

"Please don't tell me it's from these coma dreams."

"These girls were telling me Aliah had been taken to a city in Asia, maybe to be a consort for some Chinese men."

"Jesus, dude," the bartender sighed. "You need help, and I'm saying that as a friend."

"Maybe. Listen, my voice is giving out, I'll talk to you later—"

"Charlie, I'm always here...even if I don't seem like I'm listening, I am," pause. "I am really worried about you, all this shit—"

"Thanks, talk to you later," Charlie replied, hanging up the phone.

Chris' heart was in the right place but Price's instincts were telling him that his friend was wrong—Aliah *was* still out there alive, *he knew it*; Charlie would shave his beard, return to the city, and eventually find the girl...

AND NOW...
A SPECIAL PREVIEW OF CHARLIE PRICE2: SHADOW CRUISER

The young man was not expecting the needle. He had just had sex and left the girl, his mood was light, carefree—
And then something sharp was going into his neck; the young man was confused and then he was dropping his key and when bending to get them falling on his face...

He awoke naked, tied spread eagle to a mattress. His head hurt; the young man had many hangovers and this was like the worst of them. There was a bad smell, a dampness under his buttocks and between his thighs; he had soiled himself. The prisoner tried to look around, to see where he was, but his neck was also strapped in place...and then a man was to his right: White. Around forty. Slightly built. Clean shaven. Receded light brown hair. The man looked familiar, he was holding a piece of white paper in his hand.
"You know what happened to her, Safir," the man said.
"What are you doing?"Sarif sputtered, struggling against his bonds. "Where am I?"
"I need you to tell me what happened to her," the man said quietly, his face placid but his eyes watchful.
"What are you talking about, bro?"
The man took the piece of paper with both hands and swiped Safir's penis with it, the minute cut was shockingly painful and the younger man cried out. He couldn't see his dick, only feel the wound.

"What the fuck is wrong with you?" He yelled, struggling again. It only seemed to make the ropes and strap tighter.

"When I asked about your sister," the man continued in the same calm voice. "You did not act like a caring brother, that made me suspicious."

"This is about Aliah? How the fuck would I know where she is—"

And the paper swiped again; helplessly, Safir cried out. Was his cock going to be maimed?

"Your eyes, Safir," the man smiled but it was a sad smile. "You're hiding something, you may as well tell me."

Safir just stare at him hatefully, the man took the sheet of paper in both hands and readied for another swipe—

"I don't know where she is," Safir said. "That's the truth, I only delivered her."

"To whom?"

"Some Chinese dudes in a van. One of them came to me at work, he said that he liked my sister. I told him to fuck off, and he said it was worth a million dollars to me."

"A million dollars,"the man frowned. "Aliah was a cute kid but—"

"Yeah, yeah, I thought it was bullshit, too,"Safir said. "One night after work, I was walking to my car and a G wagen pulled up—

"A Mercedes SUV?"

"Yeah. The same Chinese bro was driving it, he got out and opened the hatch where there were two bags. He unzipped one, it was full of hundred dollar bills in paper bands like in the movies. I checked the bills, they were real...it had to be a million dollars in there."

"If they wanted your sister so bad, why didn't they just kidnap her?"

"I asked that,"Safir said. "They explained that cameras were everywhere; they needed someone Aliah trusted to take her out of town where they would be waiting in their van."

"So, you sold your sister for a million dollars,"the man said thoughtfully,

"I never really liked her," Safir said quietly. "I never disliked her...I guess I never felt anything. How often has someone offered you a million dollars for something that means nothing to you?"

The man had no response. Holding the piece of paper between his right index finger and thumb, he walked around the mattress once, twice, and then a third time.

"She's been missing fourteen months now,"the man said. "The odds of her being alive are low."

"I guess,"Safir said, unsure.

"Can you count to fourteen, Safir?"

The man held the sheet of paper in both hands again.

"What? Of course I can."

"Good...I need you to keep count."

He swiped Safir's penis again, the young man cried out, tears welling in his eyes.

"You'd better count, Safir, if we lost track, we start over."

"One,"the young man whimpered.

Another swipe, Safir closed his eyes and opened his mouth in a silent scream.

"Was that one, Safir?"

"No, no, it was two!"

Safir did not pass out even after the fourteenth swipe, he could feel the wetness of blood on his penis. The man was standing nearby with the sheet of paper between his right thumb and index finger. The younger man noticed that his captor was wearing gloves.

"Those are nasty cuts, Safir, we need to cleanse them."

The man dropped the paper, walked to a corner and returned with a bottle. Safir struggled against his bonds again when saw what was written on the bottle: Rubbing Alcohol.

"This might sting a little," the man smiled.

Written between 26 April 2017 and 15 September, 2021

www.ingramcontent.com/pod-product-compliance
Lightning Source LLC
Chambersburg PA
CBHW061231170626
46809CB00007B/2624